MEM KHA'S
LOVE STORY

MEM KHA'S
LOVE STORY

Jeane Kravig

"And I, brethren, when I came to you, came not with excellency of speech or of wisdom, declaring unto you the testimony of God. For I determined not to know any thing among you, save Jesus Christ, and him crucified." 1 Corinthians 2:1, 2.

PACIFIC PRESS PUBLISHING ASSOCIATION
Mountain View, California
Oshawa, Ontario

Library of Congress Cataloging in Publication Data

Kravig, Jeane
  Mem Kha's Love Story

  (Daybreak series)
  1. Kravig, Jeane. 2. Missionaries—Thailand—Biography. 3. Missionaries—United States—Biography. 4. Sev-
enth-Day Adventists—Missions—Thailand. I. Title.
BV3317.K7A35   266'.673'0924 [B]   82-2296
ISBN 0-8163-0480-7   AACR2

Contents

Glossary

BAH	Bangkok Adventist Hospital, formerly Bangkok Sanitarium and Hospital
Baht	Coin equivalent to a nickel
Farang	Foreigner
Khun	Mister or Mistress or Miss
Klong	Waterway used for transportation
Mai ben rai	Never Mind
Mem kha	A polite Thai title used in speaking to or of a woman
Phasin	Ankle-length skirt for women
Sampan	Light boat moved with one paddle
Sawaddi	Word used as a greeting or farewell
Wai	Customary Thai greeting with hands raised in a prayerlike gesture
Wat	Temple for the worship of Buddha

Prologue

The book *Mem Kha's Love Story* (*mem* meaning "ma'am" and *kha* a word indicating respect in the Thai language) would never have been written, and I would never have known the warmth and love of the charming Thai people if I had not accepted certain challenges in my life that led like rungs up a ladder.

It all started on a hot, sultry day in August when a letter arrived that turned my world upside down and inside out. "Our medical secretary is going on furlough for several months. Why not plan your trip around the world so you could stay with us and cover her home leave? Be here mid-December. Love, Helen."

I had only written to my friend, Helen Sprengel, who lived on a mission compound with her doctor husband in Thailand, that I was *thinking* of taking a trip around the world. I hadn't seriously considered it. Helen's reply came back posthaste.

I had no intentions of disrupting my well-ordered life and trotting off to what seemed to me the end of the world, namely, Thailand. Yet, in spite of my seemingly static status, a glimmer of excitement began to stir within me.

Me, the adventurous type? Hardly. My friends knew how I rolled up the rugs at night by nine or ten o'clock.

However, curled up in the safe and "sanitary" sanctuary of my living-room armchair, travel books fascinated me. Go around the world myself? I had never really entertained the thought—until now.

Images of exotic far-away places began floating through my mind—standing at the foot of snow-capped Mount Fuji in Japan, meandering in and out of fascinating shops in Hong Kong, taking a predawn boat trip to the famed floating market in Bangkok, seeing the Taj Mahal bathed in silver moonlight, walking through the massive doors of artistic cathedrals and famous museums of Europe!

My head spun, I told myself that people just don't take off on a world trip at the drop of a hat—or the arrival of a letter. Not people, that is, with a houseful of furniture, a car, and—the next thought really jolted me earthward—a mother with a cardiac problem.

But people do!

My first step was to lay before the Lord my plans of going on a trip that included Thailand. As I arose from my knees, I opened a favorite devotional book and found myself looking at a quotation from John 10:4: "He putteth forth his own sheep." Something buried in the recesses of my heart suddenly flickered to life. Me, work in a mission station? I can't say I suddenly desired to be a self-sacrificing missionary. I didn't. But a strange feeling of exhilaration swept through me, leaving a peaceful assurance that if God wanted me to work for Him a few months in Thailand, He would open the way. The focus of just taking a world trip shifted to a backseat in my mind.

Countless loose ends needed tying up before I could leave, most important of all a place for my mother to stay the year I would be gone. Miraculously, a most satisfactory room was found at the newly-opened

Ventura Estates. I could be in Thailand by mid-December!

During an evening visit with H. M. S. Richards and his wife Mabel, he made a comment that left an indelible impression on me that influenced all my later experience overseas. The Chief, as I learned to affectionately call him while working at the Voice of Prophecy, said, "Jeane, never forget that wherever you travel, you are an ambassadress for Christ. As you live among the Thai people for the next few months, take 1 Corinthians 2:1, 2 as your guide." Pastor Richards opened his Bible to the text but looked at me as he quoted the verses: "And I, brethren, when I came to you, came not with excellency of speech or of wisdom, declaring unto you the testimony of God. For I determined not to know any thing among you, save Jesus Christ, and him crucified."

Closing the Bible, Pastor Richards said, "Let us kneel down and pray that God will use you and this trip to His honor and glory."

The short dedicatory prayer of the Chief in my behalf worked—like leaven works in bread—in my heart. I felt the call and challenge of the timely text. I knew what God wanted me to be to all people at all times in my travels. What I didn't know was how drastically the experience would change me—my spiritual focus on life, my personal attachment to a foreign people, and especially my outlook on what it takes to be a missionary.

This is the story of my experience as a medical secretary on a mission hospital compound in Thailand—ten years of ups and downs and adjustments to a new life. The epilogue tells of my return to Thailand on a two-year tour as an AVSC worker, picking up the strands of those who had touched my life.

11

Meet my friends, the charming and deeply superstitious people of Thailand. When you learn about their beliefs, their customs, and their culture, you will grow to love them, as I do.

Being an ambassadress for Christ in an overseas mission was a high point of my life. I dedicate this book to those who follow me. May my experience be a guide for a happy and successful service among God's worldwide family.

Mem Kha

The city of Bangkok, known to the Thai people as Krung Thep (meaning "City of Angels"), lay wrapped in darkness when the crisp call of an unfamiliar bird awakened me. For a moment I lay in bed relishing the predawn Thai atmosphere.

Tinkling sounds, barely audible. Could they be Thai temple bells swaying to and fro in the gentle morning breeze? Suddenly, the clicking noise of a nearby *chin choak*, a small gecko, startled me as it slithered around the dark room in search of the ever-present bugs and mosquitoes for its insatiable appetite.

Again the strange bird felt obliged to make its presence known by a melodic trill, beckoning me outdoors to a world of Oriental flavor. Untangling myself from a securely tucked-in mosquito net and dressing quickly, I soon stood under some umbrellalike trees that sheltered several two-story apartment buildings lining the circle sidewalk.

Where to go? Looking around, my eyes rested on top of the four-story, concrete hospital building, less than a stone's throw away. A stairway leading to the roof had been pointed out to me while touring the building the day before. What would be better than to watch a Bangkok sunrise!

Not wanting to miss a moment of the daybreak, I ran all the way up the four double flights of stairs, pausing at the top to catch my breath. Pushing open the door to the roof of the hospital, I walked squarely into what appeared to be an outdoor kitchen on its flat surface. Several Thai women, talking among themselves with great hilarity, squatted before open charcoal fires on which pots of food were cooking.

As they became conscious of my presence, their conversation stopped; they stared at me, their eyes as curious as mine. Self-consciously, I brought the palms of my hands together and placed them under my chin in the newly learned Thai greeting. Large smiles broke out on their faces as their hands automatically returned the *wai*. Words poured out among the women, and by their hand motions I knew they were unashamedly discussing me—my hair, my skin, my clothes.

One woman, so small in stature that the top of her head barely came to my shoulder, gingerly reached out and touched my arm.

"*Mem kha*," her voice sounded soft and bell-like, "*suey*" meaning "pretty." I looked down at the petite but workworn brown hand on my arm. The gentle childish gesture not only touched my skin, it touched my heart. I knew I was going to love the Thai people.

Delighted at being alone with the Thai women, questions bubbled at the tip of my tongue, but a language barrier separated us. Remembering the sunrise, I turned away.

Meeting the Thai people stimulated my desire to see, to feel, to experience this fascinating country on my own. My feet fairly flew across the flat roof to its three-foot-high concrete ledge.

The dawn had already come and gone. Sunrays cascaded over the horizon, their golden tentacles reaching out to the city, whose buildings lay so close they resembled a great sea of shimmering rooftops. Stately, tall coconut palms jutted out from among the buildings, lifting their green fronds high in the air as though in competition with the hundreds of Thai temples, their burnished golden spires also reaching for the sky. Throughout the city, like arteries, ran golden brown canals. People in quaint one-oared sampans, gaily painted tourist launches, and overloaded barges already clogged the waterways. Slow "trishaw" taxis, noisy motor scooters, and honking buses choked the narrow roads.

From my lofty vantage point, I gazed as one mesmerized at the dazzling Oriental paradise before me.

"So this is Siam!" I half whispered to myself and to the awakening city of Bangkok.

From the back side of the hospital loomed the towering Golden Mount, a newcomer's delight for orienting himself with the city. The imposing structure tapered from a large concrete base to a thin spire in the sky; a stairway wound around it from ground level to the base of the spire. The base of the spire, I was told, housed relics of Buddha, an ancient prince-philosopher of India, now idolized in all the *wats* (temples) of Thailand. I gazed at the towering Golden Mount, not knowing that soon this Buddhist shrine would have a more personal significance in my life.

As I looked a slow procession of barefooted monks, heads shaven, their begging bowls clasped tightly to them, trudged single file down some railroad tracks in search of food. They held their flowing saffron robes closely to their sides so as not to contaminate themselves by brushing against a woman, a law of their priesthood.

There flashed into my mind a sentence from the

15

last conversation with one of my older sisters before coming to Thailand. "I can't understand why missionaries go out to disturb people who are happy and satisfied with their own culture and religion."

Were the Thai people really happy and satisfied with life as they had lived it for hundreds of generations? Certainly their smiles were broad and profuse. But what was going on in their hearts? Were they as happy inside as they appeared on the outside? Watching the monks disappear down the tracks, I wondered if I would find the answer as I mingled with the people of Thailand in the few months to come.

The sun was long up. No doubt the Sprengel family, with whom I was staying, would also be up and expecting me for breakfast. Reluctantly I took one last lingering look at the pulsating city before me, feeling that the scene would be etched in my memory forever. At last I was in old Siam, turned modern Thailand. I had read about it. Now I would live in it.

Mai Ben Rai, or Never Mind

It was my first day on the job.

As Helen and I walked into the somewhat gloomy secretarial office, I stopped and stared.

"You've got to be kidding! That's the typing chair?" I pointed to a plain straight-backed chair behind the secretarial desk.

"Jeane, you're in the mission field," Helen reminded me. "The chair is adjustable." To demonstrate her point she reached for a large medical book on a nearby shelf, placed it on the seat of my chair, and calmly announced, "Happy transcribing!"

After Helen left I stood looking out of the louvered windows, my mind ruminating on the history of the hospital.

The Bangkok Adventist Hospital (BAH) had mushroomed to the present four-story building from a small shophouse on a busy Bangkok intersection known as Five Corners. Started in 1937 by a young American doctor, Ralph Waddell, the shaky little clinic grew until in 1951 the concrete structure of the present hospital began to cast its massive shadow on a pie-shaped estate between the busy streets of Pitsanuloke and Lang Luang.

Better known all over Bangkok as the "mission hospital," BAH is also a teaching center, bringing some 150 students onto its campus. A large portion of the students come from the better schools of Bangkok and are predominantly Buddhist. A small portion of the students come from "upcountry," a term in Thailand meaning any area outside of the capital city of Bangkok.

Except for a few students coming in from neighboring countries in the Far East, the Christians attending the schools of nursing, laboratory technique, anesthesiology, and X-ray are newly baptized and mere babes in the ways of what is still considered in that part of the world a Western religion. Because of this, the social life of the missionaries stationed at BAH pivots around the students, nourishing and encouraging them to be loyal citizens of Thailand and of God. Like a powerful magnet, I immediately found myself being drawn into the constant surge of activities of the hospital.

I had daydreamed long enough. Sitting down on the rigid, straight-backed chair (the medical book becoming a literal thorn in the flesh long before the end of the day), I began to tackle the work load that had piled up. I felt my nerves fraying a bit more with each piece of hospital stationery I took out of the desk drawer. The paper was dingy, not from age but from the high humidity, and its slightly crooked letterhead baffled my sense of secretarial pride in typing perfectly centered letters on the page.

But a worse frustration confronted me that first working day, leaving me red and itching from head to toes. Mosquitoes were everywhere! And masters at their trade, these biting insects didn't make so much as a buzzing sound on attacking. Being choice bait, I later learned from experience what meant the Thai adage,

"A mosquito is to be feared more than a tiger!"

In spite of the frustrations of adjustment, I loved the flowerlike Thai people and spent a part of my evenings studying the language so I could communicate with them. Thai words are short, but it is a five-tone language, and I seemed to be almost tone-deaf! I could carry a tune and tried mastering sentences by repeating them like a song. It is this singsongy language and their small stature that gives the Thai people a childlike charm.

Like a fledgling bird, I wanted to try my wings in the Thai language. One day the opportunity came during a lunch break when a fellow missionary dropped me off at a Thai beauty shop.

In short, choppy Thai phrases I explained to the petite Thai beauty operator, "Bangs in front. Small upcurls in back."

Pleased with my prowess, I relaxed to a hair wash that consisted of four soapings, leaving my tender scalp burning from a massage administered by a pair of hands with unusually long fingernails.

Upon noticing the operator rolling the back of my hair under instead of up, I cried, "*Mai chai! Mai chai!*" I shook my head back and forth. With hands waving around my head I tried to communicate.

For a moment the operator looked confused. Then she reassuringly whispered, "*Mai ben rai* (never mind)" the magic words which seemed to be the Thai bicarbonate of soda, alleviating many an unpleasant situation a person might fall into.

My attempt at using the Thai language had failed. My charades had failed. And my confidence in communicating folded like a billowing parachute around me. The charming but persistent little operator had turned my hair style around—the back to the front.

On my way back to the office I was startled to find the words *mai ben rai* rolling around in my mind, soothing my agitated nervous system.

That evening a westering sun cast long shadows on the office walls when shattering glass interrupted my secretarial duties. Then a dull thud! Instinct brought me up out of my chair. I ran down the hospital corridor to the side door at the back where the sounds came from.

Next to the hospital building I could see a group of doctors and nurses already huddled around a person in a white hospital gown lying on the grass. A gaping hole in a louvered window on the fourth floor told the sad tale. As I watched, a nurse's aide came running with a sheet in her hands and covered the body with it. A life had gone out!

I turned to the Thai nurse standing next to me, "What happened?"

Her reply came in fairly good English. "The patient, he have cancer. Few weeks have New Year. Custom not to owe money when New Year come. Patient worry!"

I remembered seeing patients with strings tied to their wrists and ankles, hoping to drive away evil spirits. Also prayers, written with red ink on orange cloth, dangled at the end of some patients' beds. These people needed something more than their superstitious customs to hold on to. Nor would a *mai ben rai* suffice here.

How quickly the facade of this seemingly happy country began to crack before my eyes.

Thai Vignettes

The first few weeks of compound living left me feeling as though suffocated among a jungle of buildings and a mass of people. But gradually the buildings and faces began to take their allotted places in the daily pattern of life around me. I soon found myself fitting into the mission program like another cog in a great wheel that kept turning at a far more rapid pace than I had anticipated for an Oriental country.

One morning, after the office duties at the hospital had settled down to a regular routine, I tingled with excitement as Helen and I arrived at the dock at dawn to bargain for a motor launch to take us down the river on a *klong* (canal) trip.

Helen called to me, "Come on, Jeane; it's settled."

Comfortably, though somewhat noisily, we began chugging down the middle of the famous Chao Phraya, the mother of rivers in Thailand. The city of Bangkok straddles the serpentine river, and hundreds of *klongs* branch away from it creating an Oriental Venice.

Early as it was, the river seemed to be alive with people splashing in the murky water taking their morning baths. Women bathed with their *phasins* (skirts) on, modestly tied under their armpits, while babies played nude in the water around them.

"Aren't the mothers afraid the babies will drown?" I questioned.

"*Klong*side babies often can swim as soon as they learn to walk," Helen explained.

Fascinated, I watched laughing brown children in nature's garb cavort in the river like carefree dolphins, hitching rides on the sides of small barges. The stained river water served for everything—cooking, bathing, brushing teeth, washing clothes, waste disposal, and entertainment. Here the life pattern of the Thai people was going on as it probably had for hundreds of years in the past.

As we came to a junction, our eyes suddenly beheld a mass of sampans rubbing lightly together with the wash of the waves. Before us lay the famed floating market!

Caught in the congenial web, we watched the amiable confusion of hawkers and buyers busily vying with each other for the best price. The sea of boats with their smiling human cargo and bountiful foodstuffs gave the impression that these affable Thai people were without a care in the world, that their way of life was sufficient for happiness.

I looked closely into the genial faces of the people near our launch. Was that the addicting betel nut making the red stain around their lips? Were those deep lines in their faces from hidden cares and trials in their lives? The sun with its warm rays blessed the people today, but what would tomorrow hold?

All too soon it was time to leave.

A few hours later, upon returning from taking dictation in the operating room from one of the surgeons, I noticed patients and employees scurrying toward the hospital entrance. Curious, I followed them to the front steps, where a crowd already gathered.

My heart skipped a beat as I saw armed soldiers lined up on the street, facing the hospital. Was this an oft-repeated Thai coup d'etat? I glanced at the crowd around me. No one seemed alarmed but me.

Just then the manager came up beside me and asked, "Have you noticed the Thai soldiers are facing the crowd with their backs to the street?"

"Yes! But why are they here?"

He ignored my question. "Their stance in facing the people signifies something special. Oh, oh, here comes the motorcycle brigade. Watch carefully, Jeane. Here they come!"

"Here who comes?"

"The king and queen!"

My heart did a somersault! Then, a swish of a big black limousine, a glimpse of the occupants inside—His and Her Majesties of Thailand—and it was all over.

People returned to their activities laughing and chattering about the revered couple whose royal retinue at times passed in front of the hospital. The Thai people love their king and queen. Both adhere strictly to the Buddhist religion. Although polygamy is practiced throughout the small country, the stately King Bhumibol has only one wife, the beautiful Queen Sirikit.

Early that same evening I phoned Dr. Ethel Nelson, the hospital pathologist, from my office.

"We've been trying to find you, Jeane. Drop everything," Dr. Ethel ordered, but her voice sounded congenial, "and come over to our apartment immediately."

Glad to cover up the typewriter for the night, I dashed over to the quadruplex building where the Nelsons lived. On opening the door, I saw a group of missionaries gathered around the dining-room table. On the center of the table sat a large platter filled with a mound of leftover debris. It didn't take me long to sense what they had been eating. I smelled it. Durian—the large egg-shaped fruit with the hard prickly rind and soft cream-colored pulp.

I first heard about this exotic, but controversial, fruit from Dr. H. M. S. Richards in Glendale. Durian, the king of fruits in the Orient, has a reputation as strong as its odor.

"Whatever you do, Jeane," the Chief advised with a twinkle in his eyes, "taste the Oriental delicacy called durian," adding with a slight chuckle, "but be sure you have a clothespin handy for your nose."

Now Dr. Roger Nelson, a surgeon and an avid durian fan, pushed the dish of outlandish-smelling fruit over to me saying, "We saved three seeds, Jeane, for your initiation ceremony!"

All eyes watched as I bit into the custardlike meat around the seed.

"You like it!" several voices chorused together.

"I love it!" I sang out, taking another large bite and licking my lips. "I hear it has 'addicting' possibilities."

Durian tales began pouring forth. This aristocratic fruit splits families down the middle, one spouse becoming "addicted" while the other can't tolerate it in the house. As someone said, durian allows no indifference—you either love it, or you leave the room! Some liken its peculiar fragrance to rotten onions over a London sewer. In spite of my aversion to onions, I joined the durian club.

That night I crawled into bed tired but happy. However, sleep did not let down its bars, for events of the past few weeks, like vivid vignettes, kept filtering through my mind. I had never visited Europe, but I doubted that the gondola-ridden canals of Venice could surpass the festive activity of the Bangkok *klongs*. I pictured anew the pleasure-loving water populace of Thailand. I saw their amiable faces and blissful smiles, heard their carefree chatter and infectious laughter, and smelled their aromatic foods and ambrosial fruits. With every contact my love for the Thai people grew stronger. Was it their childlike ways that tugged at my heartstrings? Did their betel-nut-stained mouths and rapid chatter bespeak a lack of conscious knowledge of what lay ahead in this pilgrimage of life?

I reflected on my good fortune to be in Thailand for these few months to help the missionaries witness to this mass of humanity about Jesus' soon coming. "What a privilege!" my heart sang. But my conscience responded with, "What a responsibility!"

"And I . . . Determined. . ."

My office door opened with a flourish, and in swept a missionary friend.

"Put your typewriter to bed, Jeane," she suggested, beginning to straighten my desk, "and let's go for a dip in the sports club swimming pool. It's been miserably hot today!"

"Oh, great!" I chortled, glancing at the clock and seeing the hands nearing five. "I've perspired so much today that I could have my own private pool right here in the office, if I could collect it!"

Coming almost at the evening dinner hour, we found the swimming pool was nearly empty. After a few vigorous laps across the pool I hung languidly on the edge and enjoyed the refreshing coolness.

Three months had slipped by since I had arrived in Bangkok. The Filipino secretary on furlough would soon return. Although I hadn't met Lydia Salting, I hadn't worked long before I realized stepping into her secretarial shoes meant complete dedication to the medical duties of BAH. No job had been too menial or too hard or too long for her to do. And now, by a twist of providence, one of the other secretaries was leaving. The medical director asked if I would consider staying.

My round-the-world ticket being good for only one year, was I willing to give more of my travel time working in Bangkok? One thing I knew; if I had previously thought missionary life a staid and maybe even dull existence, I found it to be just the opposite—a most challenging, fascinating, and many-faceted life.

Soon after I stepped off the plane in mid-December, the beginning of the so-called cool season, I faced my first challenge. I discovered that Bangkok has only three climatic variations: hot, hotter, and hottest! As I lived and worked in the humid, bake-oven atmosphere, perspiration ran off me like a free-flowing rivulet, causing my clothes to cling stickily to my body. I bought some cool cotton material, and one of the Thai dressmakers that came to the compound sewed five dresses for me.

When I wore one of the new dresses, a student nurse daintily fingered the soft material. "*Mem kha*, you dress is pretty."

I smiled at her broken English and her difficulty in pronouncing the r's. Feeling pleased at her remark, I explained, "The material is cotton and comfortable for the hot weather here in Bangkok."

Her next words startled me. "You lucky. You no sleeves. Cool, yes?"

I knew the student nurse's uniform consisted of a pinafore over a short-sleeved dress. Now I noticed the small group of students around me all wore sleeves in their off-duty dresses as well.

I hesitated, then spoke slowly so they would be sure to understand, "Do you wear sleeves in your dresses because you have to?"

"Yes," came several replies.

The student who fingered my dress again spoke up, "*Mem kha*, the dean say rule of school!"

Another voice in the group of girls before me chimed in, "The dean say sleeveless dresses not nice for Christian girls."

Was I hearing a decided emphasis to the remark? "The dean say" seemed to hold a lot of weight in the girls' opinion, and veiled behind thick black lashes, the unreadable almond eyes of the students waited for my reaction.

My mind raced at computer speed. Here were Buddhist girls having to live up to Christian dress standards. Surely, my mind reasoned, the school's dress rules of modesty should not be different from that of the missionaries. For the sake of my own convenience and comfort would I compromise on the rule of Christian decorum and create a double standard on the hospital compound?

Pastor Richard's advice on being an ambassadress and the text he gave flashed into my mind. "And I, brethren, . . . determined not to know any thing among you, save Jesus Christ, and him crucified." I knew what I must do.

The Thai dressmaker found barely enough leftover material to have sleeves put in three dresses. Nevertheless, I felt, in the light of principle, the loss of two dresses would someday prove a gain. And it did. Sooner than I expected.

When I met Dr. Ethel a few days later she remarked about the dress I wore—wasn't it sleeveless the last time she saw it? She was a full-time missionary; and who was I, just a fill-in for a few months, to tell her about what I thought as an inconsistency among us missionaries. Still, I felt she might understand.

Dr. Ethel's eyebrows knit together slightly in meditative concentration as I related my conversation with the group of nursing students. When I finished, her

28

words came slowly, "Jeane, you've given me a new thought. I've been bothered about my influence in wearing sleeveless dresses, knowing the dormitory rules." She paused a moment, then added, "I'll join you. Then I'll feel better about the matter."

Now, as my feet kicked up the pool's cool water and I watched the sunrays form mini-rainbows in the spray, almost unconsciously my reflective thoughts began formulating a decision in my mind regarding staying on at the hospital.

Missionary life enthralled me. In the States I had been a follower, not a leader. But life in Thailand turned me around, not by choice but by necessity. One *had* to be a leader to help carry forward the many facets of the mission, chief among these being the spiritual. From the experiences around me, I realized these very pressures brought out the best or the worst in the missionary. And for one who had never aspired to missionary status, God had subtly brought out talents I never knew I possessed! I liked the challenge of missionary life, the challenge to live bigger than my puny self. I knew I would stay on with the secretarial duties of the hospital for the remainder of the year.

Childish screams interrupted the serenity of my thoughts. A boy, about seven years of age, dressed only in a ragged pair of short khaki pants, zigzagged madly across the lawn toward the back wall of the pool as a white-coated attendant from the sports club dashed after him with a long stick in his hands. With the alacrity of a jungle monkey, the dark-skinned urchin scaled the fence crying out each time the stick fell on him, "*Bai laow! Bai laow!*"

The little rogue dropped over the top of the wall, and I sighed with relief at his escape. Turning to look for my co-worker and finding her nearby, I queried,

29

"Whatever was the boy shouting?"

"*Bai* means 'gone' and *laow* means 'already,' " she explained. "*Bai laow*—gone already!"

We chuckled at the apropos expression, and then I questioned, "Do you suppose he wanted a free swim in the pool?"

"With all the *klongs* around? Most likely he came to *kamoi* [steal] personal property from the changing rooms." My friend's eyes scanned the horizon. "The sun is sinking fast, Jeane. We'd better be getting back to the compound."

Pra Maha Samruay

The air in the dining room became more oppressive as an early-evening monsoon beat against the house, causing the wooden shutters to rattle against their moorings. No doorbell had rung. Nor had I heard the screen door at the top of the landing open or shut. Nevertheless, as I read the newspaper at the dining-room table, I felt a presence near me and glancing up saw a man noiselessly approaching.

"Oh!" I gasped. Then, recognizing my visitor, let out a breath of relief, at the same time wondering if I would ever get used to the Thai way of entering a house without knocking.

A young-appearing barefooted man stopped a few feet away, one hand behind him holding back the flowing folds of a saffron robe. Black almond eyes, wide open yet unfathomable, peered out of a round face. His close-shaven head now cocked in birdlike fashion as if in inquiry.

Dropping his hold on the robe, the young priest greeted me with a Thai *wai*.

I mumbled a confused Thai greeting, adding, "Forgive me, but you startled me. You have come to study?"

Now the priest looked puzzled. I realized my rapid

English sentences fell on his ears the same way as a burst of the Thai language entered my own—an unintelligible mass of sounds.

"Study?"

A thin smile of understanding spread over his face.

"Come." I motioned him to follow me and walked through the living room toward the sun porch. He hesitated, then followed me, his head pivoting as though looking for someone in the room.

In the sun-room I sat down at the small table, motioning the monk to do the same. But he continued to stand as he unloaded a Bible-story book, Voice of Prophecy lessons, and a pencil from a saffron cloth begging bag that hung over his shoulder, his eyes still searching the other room. Just then Helen came out of her bedroom and, having met the priest before, called out a Thai greeting as she picked up the newspaper and settled down on the living-room sofa. A big smile spread over the priest's face, and an audible sigh escaped his lips as he sat down at the table across from me. He seemed peculiarly happy about something and began to rattle away in very broken English garbled with a Thai accent.

It was now my turn to slow him down. "Speak slowly—*cha cha!*"

"In *wat* have rule. No be alone with woman." He giggled and looked at Helen's stabilizing presence in the living room.

Seeing the name *Pra Maha* Samruay on one of his Voice of Prophecy lessons, I pointed to the name and asked, "Have meaning?"

"Oh yes!" he proudly answered. "*Pra* mean 'priest.' *Maha* mean 'great.' Samruay mean 'rich'!" Without warning laughter burst forth from the young priest's lips. "Ha, ha, ha!"

Not comprehending his great mirth in the meaning of his name, I asked, "Then in English you are called the great, rich priest?"

Nodding his head up and down, his laughter now somewhat controlled, the monk kept repeating, "Wonderful! Wonderful!"

A missionary family that arrived in Thailand about the same time as I did met *Pra Maha* Samruay at a temple. Soon after, they began studying English with him from a Bible-story book, as well as from the Voice of Prophecy lessons. So that the priest could better understand the meaning of the Bible lessons, and not just use them to further his study of English, they also enrolled him in the Thai Bible course. After a few months in Bangkok, the family left for their upcountry mission station. Dr. Ethel agreed to pick up the studies with the monk. An avid student, the priest asked to study four nights a week. Not having the time to give him, Dr. Ethel invited me to share two nights of the study time.

Study with a Buddhist priest? What better way could I gain an insight into the culture and character of the Thai people, whose passage from birth to death is inseparable from the *wat*. And who knows what impact the story of Jesus would have on the young priest.

That first day our study progressed slowly because of the language barrier. As Samruay read from the Bible-story book, I soon discovered that his reading ability far surpassed his speaking ability of the English language. I could answer his questions about the Bible story better by writing a few words on paper than by a verbal explanation. I also noticed that no matter how often I asked to use his pencil or reached for it from his hand, he always managed to first lay it down quickly on the table. Finally it got through to me that

33

he would not hand the pencil to me directly.

"Why?" I questioned.

"*Wat* rule. No touch woman."

"But, Samruay, you no touch me," I contradicted. "You touch pencil."

Samruay only shook his head back and forth repeating, "*Wat* rule. Have *wat* rule."

A few nights later Dr. Ethel and I lingered outside her apartment. Handing me a sheet of paper from the manila folder in her hand, Ethel said, "Read this, Jeane. It's a short theme I asked Samruay to write on his life. It will give you an insight into his background and reason for becoming a monk."

Reaching for the sheet of paper, I moved closer to the light shining from the front porch of the apartment and began reading:

"Story of My Life"

"My name is Samruay. I was born at Ayudhaya. I have sad thing happen in my life the first time I was born. I never seen my father. I ask, Mother, who is my father? Where is he? She never answered.

"When I grow up I help feed the buffalo and planted rice. I sleep on top of buffalo. Oh, very hard!

"Mother remarry when I am twelve. The man not kind, drank and smoked opium. Mother work in jungle cutting wood to sell.

"When fourteen I had met a second sad thing. Mother died of malaria. O God, how could I do? I decide I not be stupid all my life. God guide me to Buddhist *wat*. Here priest taught children. The priest let me stay with him at the *wat* three years and can read and write Thai language. Then I left to Bangkok for more education, where I stay four years as a novice. Then I became a priest at Wat Sakhet."

Looking up at Ethel I asked, "Wat Sakhet, what temple is that?"

"In English it's called the Golden Mount—not too far away from here."

The Golden Mount? That was the temple I saw from the hospital rooftop soon after arriving in Thailand, the spire of its pagoda "high and lifted up"! With added interest I went back to reading:

"I learn Bali, Thai, and a little English. I know English from the Christian people. Nine years ago I lost Mother. Now have father, mother, sisters, and brothers. How did I feel now? Oh! Very happy!"

I asked Ethel, "Father and mother? Dr. Roger and you?"

"Yep, guess so!" she quipped. "You're in there too."

"One of the sisters, I take it."

Ethel nodded as I handed the paper back to her, repeating the monk's name softly, "*Pra Maha* Samruay, the great, rich priest!" No wonder Samruay laughed so hard when he told me the meaning of his name. Great? Rich? With that background? Only, I felt he shouldn't have laughed; he should have cried! I found the Thai people often laughed when tears seemed more appropriate, an emotional cover-up of embarrassment closely related to their verbal *mai ben rai*.

"What a pathetic background," I finally said. "But, Ethel, Samruay's theme indicates a spiritual leaning toward God, even at the age of fourteen. He has come a long, long way! He writes and spells exceptionally well in English, much better than he talks."

"The verbal use of any foreign language is usually hardest. Now, listen to this. I've invited Samruay to take the laboratory course here at the hospital.''

"And leave the priesthood?'' I gasped.

"Well, he could hardly do it in a saffron robe!''

"Oh, of course not,'' I agreed. "Is he interested?''

"So much so he is coming in to take an aptitude test.''

The Pampered Priest

It was late fall and monsoons drenched the Thai world daily. Lightning streaked across the sky, and buildings trembled as thunder cracked sharply in a fit of Thai temper, rolling angrily away in long, indignant growls. And then the rain poured down like cascading waterfalls gone berserk, hitting the sun-baked sod and turning the Oriental world into a huge steam bath. Abruptly, fingers of sun broke through patches of blue sky.

Changes came quickly in the Orient, not only in the weather but among the hospital personnel as well. A new medical director, Dr. Louis Ludington, arrived. With the new director came more changes, most radical of all his suggestion that I stay on as a permanent member of the BAH team.

"But my mother—"

"Bring her here," Dr. Ludington interrupted.

"My mother? She's a serious cardiac patient!"

A slow smile, Dr. Louis' trademark, crossed his face. "I'm a heart surgeon, and so is Dr. Nelson. Where could she be better off than right on a hospital compound?"

I had fallen hopelessly in love with mission life, yet I felt reticent to ask Mother, at seventy-five years of age, to leave family, friends, and her familiar way of life. It was with a great deal of trepidation that I wrote the letter of invitation. "They've asked me to stay on as a regular missionary, Mother, and invited you to come to Bangkok. Do you think you could come?"

The constant flow of work in the secretarial office kept my fingers dancing over the typewriter keys. In addition to the daily work load, the medical director asked me to work out a public relations course for the employees. Unintentionally, hospital personnel were adding insult to injury when asking even obviously pregnant patients, "What your disease?" Immersed in my new task when someone tapped me on the shoulder, I spun around on my newly acquired typewriter chair in surprise.

"Sorry to frighten you, Jeane," Dr. Ethel's familiar voice reassured me, "but Samruay is here to take his test for entering the lab course. We dropped by for a word of prayer first."

After prayer Ethel asked, "Samruay, do you want to tell about your friend's strange dream?"

A big smile broke out on the priest's face. "Oh yes! I have plan to ask woman who feed me rice, 'Shall I become "man" [non-priest].' But woman, Boon Mi, say first, 'I see you "man" in my sleep last night!' Oh, very wonderful!" Samruay's favorite phrase expressed his genuine amazement.

Ethel stated more than she asked, "You, of course, left your idols at home, Samruay."

"Have all!" The priest patted his begging bag, a Bible-story book peeking out.

"Those idols can't help you," Dr. Ethel commented.

"I know," the young monk rejoined. "Don't speak, do they?"

"Even that Bible-story book can't help you, Samruay. Why not leave it and the charms here with me," I encouraged.

"Yes," Samruay agreed, "after test."

"Now, Samruay," Ethel continued, "put your faith in God, not idols."

Somewhat reluctantly Samruay placed his idols on my desk, then said, "Trust God," and followed Dr. Ethel out of the room. A moment later he reappeared. "Leave book too!" A flicker of triumph crossed his face as he placed the Bible-story book on my desk.

Curious, I examined the lifeless idols—a triangular ebony charm with a Buddha engraved on it, a gold-colored metal Buddha, and a tiny ivory image. Fingering the ivory talisman, I discovered the top unscrewed to reveal a fragile, minutely carved Buddha hidden inside. The man-made idols lying on my desk appeared harmless, and little did I then realize that these charms masked a power strong as steel, holding its victim relentlessly in superstition.

Several hours later Dr. Ethel dropped by my office.

"How did Samruay do?" I burst out, searching her face for a clue.

"Hmmmm!" Ethel murmured with a shrug of her shoulders, her nonchalance revealing nothing. Then she smiled. "He passed. He's finishing some paper work in the classroom. If you have his charms and Bible-story book handy, I'll take them to him."

The monsoons gradually emptied themselves out, and on their heels brisk winds blew down from the snow-covered Russian steppes, fanning away, for brief spells, the torrid heat.

I was now living by myself in a newly decorated apartment while the usual occupant went on furlough. I missed the congenial atmosphere of the Sprengel household, where Wan Di, the cook, mincing about bashfully on her bare feet, ingratiated herself with everyone through her shy smile and superb culinary instinct. But my new independence afforded me other advantages. Several overseas nursing students had requested that I become their guardian, and I now was in a position to handle this new responsibility.

One Sunday soon after changing apartments, from my kitchen window I saw a procession of people slowly making their way to the circle walk—a youthful Thai man followed in single file by five Thai women. Then I recognized the man—Samruay!

The incessant jangling of my phone called me from the window. Ethel's voice, ordinarily calm, sounded excited. "Jeane, do come over immediately. Samruay's left the priesthood!"

As I entered the Nelson's living room, Samruay came toward me, dropped respectfully to his knees and bowed several times before rising. He appeared ill at ease, dressed for the first time since childhood as a commoner. The garb he had chosen consisted of an immaculate white shirt and trousers, his black leather belt and shiny black shoes contrasting sharply. Black and white, colors worn in the Orient for auspicious occasions, revealed inner feelings regarding the significance of Samruay's leaving the priesthood and becoming a plain "man." Black hair grown out to a crew-cut length now crowned his normally shaved head.

"These my mothers." Samruay's hand swept toward the five small women demurely sharing the living-room couch. "Feed me *twice* every day." This was especially significant, since monks normally eat only once each day.

Their plain clothes bespoke a humble existence, and yet for five years these faithful Buddhist women had revered the young boy priest and shared their meager fare. Impressed by their daily sacrifice on behalf of their religious requirements, I greeted the women with a respectful Thai *wai*. Then turning to Samruay, I slowly asked, "Which woman had the dream that you would become a 'man'?"

"Oh, wonderful! Boon Mi." Samruay pointed to a pleasant-faced woman sitting in the middle of the group. "She old one. Sixty!" Boon Mi smiled, sensing we were discussing her. Talking so frankly about her age embarrassed me. However, I was learning that the Thai people had few inhibitions and spoke openly on most every subject.

"Samruay good priest?" I asked, looking at Boon Mi. Her eyebrows puckered together and, remembering, I asked Samruay to translate. He balked, but prodded by Dr. Ethel, Samruay turned to Boon Mi and began talking rapidly in Thai. Soon the other four women jumped into the conversation, their chatter, bouncing back and forth like a tennis ball, began to sound like a family squabble.

A sheepish grin appeared on Samruay's face as he turned back to me and said, "Sometimes not keep rice. Empty begging bowl out on ground." Samruay shook his head back and forth, his eyes downcast. "Oh, very bad of me!"

We laughed at the unwilling confession, but I surmised Samruay's temper tantrums must have been very disconcerting to the women. Feeding the monk meant merit for the next life, according to the Buddhist teaching, and in refusing the rice, the temperamental priest depreciated the quality of their gift.

Dr. Ethel examined one of the women for dizzy spells, giving her some sample medicine. Then the women arose, lifted their hands in the Thai *wai*, and started walking to the door. Samruay prostrated himself in front of them, his head bowed low and the palms of his hands together, held high on his forehead in heartfelt respect. From the eyes of the former priest large tears fell to the floor. The Buddhist women looked at the kneeling monk, now turned "man." Their own eyes welled up with tears as they turned away and silently walked out the door.

Samruay stood up. Tears still flowing from an unlatched heart, he lingered by the porch screen door and watched the women parade down the circle and out of the routine of his familiar life—a life of rising before daybreak, begging food, and not eating after twelve noon.

The poignant scene had brought tears to both Ethel's and my eyes, for we had grown fond of the young monk whose human nature yearned for earthly family ties. When starting to make plans to leave the priesthood, Samruay had no clothes, no shoes, no money, nothing that would help him fit into a world outside the Buddhist monkhood. And even if we gave him money, he could not go and buy the things he needed, due to temple rules. Having never worn ordinary clothes, Samruay didn't know his sizes. Nor could we, being women, touch the saffron-robed monk to measure him. Buying an outfit for the monk, while guessing at the sizes, provided a strange shopping spree!

Dr. Ethel walked over to Samruay and put her hand lightly on his shoulder. "Samruay, we're glad you're here! I'll call a couple of lab boys to help carry your things over to the dormitory."

Ethel and I watched the boys walking away, the new "man" shouldering the heaviest box. Neither of us spoke, remembering the tender scene of parting and pondering the future of the former saffron-robed priest. Would the many Buddhist students and employees accept his coming out of the *wat* to a Christian institution? Or would they surreptitiously persecute him? Regardless of hospital rules not to act derogatorily toward Christianity, strong Buddhist personalities in the various medical classes had, in the past, banded students together in an oath not to accept the Western religion.

I broke the silence. "Has a monk ever left the priesthood and come to study at the hospital before?"

"No, not a regular priest," Ethel answered, her eyes still following the retreating procession. "Every good Buddhist man in Thailand goes into the priesthood sometime in his life for three months. Our male Buddhist employees take time off to do this." Dr. Ethel paused, then went on speaking, "Samruay wanted to leave the priesthood, and the lab course will give him a profession whereby he can earn a livelihood in the outside world."

I hesitated asking my next question. "Do you think Samruay can survive the students' questionings and barrage of remarks that are sure to come?"

Ethel shrugged her shoulders. "We'll just have to wait and see."

Pattaya by the Sea

Upon request I agreed to drive a Volkswagon busload of students to the beach village of Pattaya, an idyllic setting for the Christian Fellowship retreat. I ignored the thoughts of the VW's stick shift or of having to drive on the left side of the road.

Now, Pattaya bound, the students' garbled chatter, a mixture of Thai and English, sounded like a rollicking scherzo to my ears. The weekend at Pattaya provided an anticipated feast of the soul for the students.

The Fellowship meetings were open to anyone on the hospital compound, but the special weekend retreats were mainly for the Christians and those showing a decided interest. A little controversy arose over this practice, as some missionaries felt it discriminated against the Buddhist students. Nonetheless, it seemed necessary to strengthen the small minority of Christians whose witness was constantly being diluted among the vast majority of Buddhist students. Dormitory roommates were set up so a Christian student lived with a Buddhist, and these toddlers in the faith found it an uphill struggle to grow and mature in such an environment. They needed a time to come apart from the others and renew their spiritual direction with fellow believers. These retreats filled that need.

Soon after leaving Bangkok's erratic traffic, the highway trailed alongside the wave-lapped shores of the Gulf of Siam. The students settled down and began singing Christian choruses in Thai, their high-pitched, bell-like voices giving the familiar airs an Oriental sweetness. Without warning, a stout odor intruded on the VW. The singing faded away, and the students began to giggle.

"Smell from what?" I questioned in simple English.

"Fish town!" chorused several voices. "Chintara live here!" Fingers pointed to an attractive student whose dimples shyly played hide-and-seek in response to the students' antics. Chintara was a Christian of another faith and a good influence in the dormitory. Through the VW's rearview mirror I cast her a quick smile of understanding.

It was late afternoon when we reached Pattaya and its most attractive asset, a crescent-shaped beach with an exotic backdrop of stately coconut trees. Here our weekend retreat would be held at the bougainvillea-splashed Baptist camp, whose facilities included a main dormitory, some cabins, and a dining hall.

After a short swim and a tasty rice supper, we sat around the tables in the dining hall, singing Thai songs to begin sundown worship. Leading out in the evening meeting fell on my shoulders, and after a devotional thought, I turned the meeting into a testimonial channel.

Recently baptized Chanarong, a lab student with mischievous black eyes and a beguiling smile, stood and gave his testimony. His animated Thai led me to hastily ask a Thai teacher sitting next to me to translate what he was saying. In a subdued whisper she complied.

"My turning to Jesus come through discipline problem. Thai people great sport fans; parades often block streets off two to three hours. I love sports too, but most games on Sabbath. Cannot attend 'cause rule of school. But one Sabbath, cannot resist. I escape from compound and march in parade carrying big banner. When passing Chinese church my eyes cannot believe what they see: My boss and teacher, Dr. Ethel, waiting for parade to go by! Too late to duck behind banner, our eyes met already. Later she punish by giving me a Bible study on the Sabbath. Then have to write up paper on the subject. For the first time I understand truth. I keep studying the Bible. Now give energy for sports to Jesus.''

Sanoh, a quiet-voiced nursing student, arose and told of the conflict many students go through when accepting Christ. She spoke in English more distinctly than the usual Thai student.

"I was raised a Buddhist. Now and then I heard name of Jesus, but did not like as I always heard when something bad happen. Later I know I hear it only as bad language.

"I came to Bangkok and went to English Christian school that keep Sunday as holy day. Here we have to study Bible.

"The school have revival service. At end of meeting each row march up, and if wished to make decision, student step aside at front and into other group. I really want to step aside. But each time my friends, they love me very much, gang up on me and push me along."

Sanoh's words "my friends, they love me very much" rolled around in my mind. Here lay the crux of the difficulty a loving Thai faces in trying to accept Jesus—an unsheathed sword that would separate him from his friends. My thoughts strayed to my growing friendship with the student nurse Nara. Nara's heart reached out for Christ, but her close friendship with a Buddhist roommate held Nara back.

The price of accepting Christianity in Thailand is high. Buddhism is not only taught as a state religion in the school system, but also the student takes an oath that is meant to tie him to the government religion for life. Every school day Thai students attend an impressive flag-raising ceremony. As the fluttering flag reaches its zenith, the air swells with student voices singing the slow but stately Thai anthem, whose words proclaim fealty to the Lord Buddha:

> Kha wora Pootta Chao
> ao mano lae sira kran
> nob Phra-phumi ban boonya
> direk
> ek baromma Chakarin
> Phra Sayamin
> Phra-yodsa ying yong
> Yen sira pro Phra-boriban
> Pon Phra-kunta raksa
> puang pracha pen sooksarn
> Khor bandarn
> ta prasong dy
> jong sarit
> dang wang wora hareutai
> duja tawai chai chaiyo

> I, slave of the Lord Buddha
> prostrate my heart and head
> to pay homage and give great
> blessings to the Protector of the land,
> one of the great Chakri Dynasty,
> Head of the Thai people,
> supreme in rank.

I draw comfort from your protection.
Because of your gracious care
all the people are happy and peaceful.
We pray
that whatever you wish for
fate will grant you,
according to your heart's desire,
to bring you prosperity. We salute you!

Sanoh's voice pentrated my thoughts as she finished speaking. "When I start nurse's training at BAH, I learn about true Sabbath keeping. At last I decide to make my stand for Jesus."

Outside rain beat monotonously on the roof, but inside a sweet spirit fell on our Christian group, hovering tenderly over the meeting, uniting us together as one in Christ.

Early Sunday morning we left Pattaya. The students' bodies ached from an overdose of exercise, but their souls were satisfied from partaking bountifully of a real spiritual feed. I was especially content; I had slept, played, and prayed with a part of God's family in Thailand. As I backed the VW into its stall at the hospital compound, I sensed a little better the knotty problems facing the Thai people in coming to Jesus.

Around the World . . . And Back!

Less than a year, and the mission field had captured my heart, metamorphosed my life, and molded me into a willing slave for Christ! Paradoxically, I felt liberated. It wasn't that I suddenly sprouted wings. In fact, beginning to see myself as I really was—an image bulky with self—I stood on the fringe of realizing the truth of Jesus' proposition: "Learn of me; . . . for my yoke is easy, and my burden is light."

I admired the Bangkok missionaries. They lived together like one big family, grappling with problems, disagreeing, and, yes, sometimes even squabbling, but still loving one another. Whether you were a part of the organized work or just a traveler as I, passing through, they treasured you like one of them. How I loved them! And, lingering ever bigger in the back of my mind was the question, How could I ever leave them? Or, could Mother ever come so far over here?

Then her reply came through in her typical unadorned way, "Of course I could!" I hugged the letter of emancipation to me, miniature rainbows glistening on my eyelashes. My novice missionary experience was about to blossom into a bona fide misionary status!

While I was preparing for home leave, the medical director called me into his office. "Jeane, the House

49

Committee voted for you to be the acting dean in the nursing student's dormitory when you return from America."

"Acting dean? Me? Why, I've never been a dean!"

Dr. Louis smiled. "Just for a year, Jeane, while Miss Feltus is away on home leave."

"But what about my mother? The dean's apartment is on the second floor, and with her heart problem, she can't climb stairs."

"If you'll agree to be acting dean, we'll work that out when you get back. *Khun* [Mr. or Mrs. or Miss] Vanna will stay on as your assistant. She lives in the dormitory. I'm sure she'll be a real help to you."

My mind, benumbed by the turn of events, refused to function beyond the fact that I was a medical secretary, *not* a dean! Then, like a warning signal, a phrase began flashing through it, "not to know any thing among you, save Jesus Christ, *and him crucified*!"

The medical director was waiting for my answer. In a voice barely audible, I mumbled, "If you think I can do the job, I'm willing."

Packing . . . visitors . . . packing . . . phone calls . . . packing. Suitcases, clothes, and packages strewn over furniture and floor. The place was in chaos, and I had to leave in a few hours!

Later that day an enormous metal bird rose powerfully into the air, slicing through puffball clouds scudding along in the Thai-blue sky. I let out a big sigh—I had made it! Belted into a seat in the jet's colorful interior, I tried to relax, but wound up like a coiled spring, I couldn't rein in my meandering mind. I let it wander.

The day started at dawn for me when Vi and Kim dropped in to say good-bye before going on early-morning duty. Being guardian to these two Oriental girls had often challenged my ingenuity in trying to help solve their youthful frustrations.

After the girls left, Nara, now in her fourth year of nursing, brought me her farewell gift—a beautiful Thai lei. Sensing why Nara stayed on the fringes of accepting Christ and played her own game of hide-and-seek with God, I boldly asked, "Nara, would you like to change roommates?"

A sadness crept into her black eyes, and she slowly shook her head. I had touched the problem. A quiet girl, Nara submerged her identity vicariously in her roommate's more dazzling personality—popular, smart, president of her class—but also covertly anti-Christian. Under her roommate's spell, Nara was gambling with her own eternal destiny.

As the jet droned on toward India, I unclasped the seat belt and settled more comfortably into my place. My thoughts continued to entwine the people I had come to know and to love.

Soon after lunch I heard the screen door creak gently and knew from their mode of entry, that my knockless visitor was Thai.

"*Sawaddi*," I called out. "I'm in the bedroom."

Chintara, with the shy dimples, stood in the doorway. Dropping to her knees by my chair, in Oriental respect she bent her head toward my left shoulder, the palms of her slender hands placed together near her forehead.

"*Mem kha*," her songlike voice trembled slightly, "all you teach me, I remember and believe. Sabbath too." Soft almond-shaped eyes filled with tears, but dimples surfaced as she spoke.

The Bible studies with Chintara had not been in vain. Her going-away "gift" far outrivaled all others, and my heart beat in a gladsome rhythm.

The lab students had come en masse to the airport, Samruay among them. His adjustments to the gregarious compound life had been wobbling up and down like a yo-yo. Missing from the dormitory one night, he was found sleeping in his old room in the temple grounds. "Too noisy on compound," was all he would say.

With one foot still in the *wat*, his study habits fluctuated according to his moods. Samruay had the brains, but his heart wasn't in it. Could it be that our fears for him had turned into facts? Persecution spurted from students and employees, so cleverly camouflaged you couldn't quite put your finger on it to take action—someone standing alongside Samruay humming "The Yellow Priest," a Thai song about a turncoat monk. Samruay disloyal to Thailand? They were touching a vulnerable spot!

Headed for home, I felt my spirit reach back to the delicate, flowerlike Thai people. "Please, God, help them!" my heart cried. "Please draw the people of Thailand into the freedom of eternal truth!"

Time in the homeland passed by uneventfully until I received a letter from Helen the Friday before returning to Thailand. Devouring the morsels of news, my eyes stopped abruptly at a small paragraph near the end:

"We've started a campaign for funds to renovate the compound church. The student dormitory has been asked to raise $500; this responsibility will fall on the acting dean."

I had almost forgotten I was the acting dean. I was also probably the world's worst fund raiser. Helen's next sentence—"The majority of students in the dorm come from poor families, so maybe you should try to raise as much as possible there in the States"—

sent me to my knees. "O God, you know I leave next week! I have only one more Sabbath appointment. Please, God, help me somehow, someway, to at least raise $300 of the students' goal." I hesitated to say Thank You, but I didn't dare let my weak faith stand between me and the solution to this crisis. I breathed a thin "Thank You, Lord."

Sabbath morning, sitting on the platform of my home church in Glendale, California, I silently reminded myself, "It's not proper to solicit, Jeane; just state the facts." I stood up to speak.

Describing my newly adopted country of Thailand and the tremendous spiritual needs, my words rolled out fluently. The humble compound church came alive, even to me, as I verbally portrayed the board shutters at the window openings, the slatted seats cutting into the flesh long before the church service ended, and the students, Christian and Buddhist, sitting on the front benches each Sabbath morning, clothed sometimes in faded, but clean, cotton dresses. Barely touching on the plan to renovate the church, I sat down.

At the close of church, people began handing me money for Thailand. Later, checks came pouring in, until the amount reached not only $300, not even the necessary $500 goal, but $1300!

With my heart sensitive to the magnitude of God's liberality, I cried, "O God, my faith was so puny—only $300! How could I have doubted Your great generosity, Your blessings?" (The church treasurer called to tell me it was one of the largest offerings ever received in that church.) My heart, flooding with a mixed blessing of humility and thankfulness, could not have contained what God still had to reveal to me about the matter.

Across from the student-nurses' dormitory a one-bedroom, ground-floor apartment awaited Mother and me on the hospital compound. I stood peering apprehensively through the living-room windows at the three-story dormitory building. How I shrank from the thoughts of crossing the lawn to take up my duties as the *mae bahn* (housemother) of 120 lively Oriental girls. Then a shaft of light pierced through my wall of dread—the three entrances to the dormitory faced my apartment!

"What a disadvantage to any recalcitrant student," I laughed, shaking my head in mock dismay, "but what a vantage point for the new acting dean!"

Mae Bahn (Housemother)

Before me sat most of the 120 dormitory students, all with shiny jet black hair and dark inquisitive eyes. As I began reading off the study-hall roll call, suppressed laughter broke out around the room. Though outwardly calm, chaos reigned within my heart. Then the reason for the students' tittering dawned on me— my wrong tones in pronouncing their names must be giving them a hilarious meaning! Relaxed, I began smiling with the students.

Study period over and the lights-out bell bringing the buzzing dormitory to an abrupt halt, I began to check halls. All seemed quiet until I started down the stairs to the second floor. I heard muffled laughter coming from a room at the end of the long hall. With a tap on the door and a quick entry, I startled a group of Bangkok girls sitting cross-legged on the floor enjoying a feast of food. Having indulged in midnight feeds myself during dormitory days, I was inclined to not only overlook their breaking of rules, but even to join them! But now my role was changed: I was the upholder of rules.

"Girls," I spoke slowly so they could understand, "I'll have to fine you for having food in the dormitory and most of you for being out of your rooms after lights out. This will cost you one hundred *baht*." I knew the city girls had more money than the upcountry students, and a dollar fine would not be too hard for this group.

I forgot about the fine until several days later when one of the students came into the office and, smiling, handed me a hundred-*baht* bill. The assistant dean, sitting on the couch, asked, "What for the *baht*?"

I told her of the fine, adding, "I felt, *Khun* Vanna, the Bangkok girls could scrape up a dollar among them."

"*Mem kha*, one hundred *baht* is *five* dollars your money!"

"Oh, no, *Khun* Vanna!" I was appalled at my error in Thai currency and to think the group of Buddhist girls, almost a clique, had been even friendlier to me after the incident! When I tried to return eighty *baht*, they only laughed and refused. Each of the Oriental girls in the dormitory began to take on a personal identity, and, like a jewelry box of precious gems, each was different with her own special luster.

However, I found supervising students a far cry from manipulating a mechanical typewriter. The Oriental philosophy, it seems, makes getting caught, not the misconduct, the face-losing factor. Vanna's assistance in the dean's office proved invaluable as she arbitrated between my direct American ways and the more roundabout ways of the Thai students. In the short time I'd worked with Vanna, I had grown very fond of her.

A little taller than the average Thai woman, Vanna had an extrovert personality with a fetching way of expressing her opinions in English. She had never heard of God or Jesus until she came to BAH. Vanna became a Christian while a student nurse for two reasons: First, she admired her American teachers; and, second, every Sabbath afternoon she loved to take a nap, but someone always called her for Bible study. So, she reasoned, if she was baptized they wouldn't call her anymore! However, basically a conscientious person, Vanna, as she learned more of the religion she'd embraced, became a truly converted Christian.

One evening I asked Vanna to help me buy some fruit outside the back gate. Looking the luscious fruit over, Vanna shook her head and spoke a few words in Thai. Outside the shophouse I turned to Vanna.

"Did you tell the woman we'd not buy the fruit because of no room in the refrigerator?"

"Oh, white lie. Price too high." Vanna grinned. "Not want to hurt feelings."

Beginning to understand the reluctance of the sensitive Thai nature to face an issue head on, I explained to Vanna that I, too, had grappled with the same problem, only to find there is no such thing as a "white" lie. Having settled the issue satisfactorily, our fruit bought, and back again in the dean's office, Vanna turned to settle an unknowing account with me.

"*Mem kha*, how come you put Mother in front seat when go in car? Front seat for driver and unimportant person."

I chuckled. "In America, *Khun* Vanna, people cannot afford a chauffeur. The front seat next to the driver is considered the best seat because it gives the best view." Satisfied, Vanna arose from the couch to leave. "Oh, one more thing, *Khun* Vanna, the $500 goal the dormitory has been asked to raise for renovating the church. Any suggestions as to how we'll raise it?"

As Vanna sat down again, a self-satisfied feeling crept over me. I thought of the money I'd already turned over to the building committee. I had asked that it not be mentioned until after the students made some effort toward reaching the goal themselves.

"*Mem kha*, most students come from poor family. And not Christian too! Is big goal!"

"I know, *Khun* Vanna, but have you any idea of how to start?"

Vanna's eyes shifted to the floor. Finally she spoke, her voice subdued by the weighty task, "I will write Thai letter for student to take parent, asking for donation. Some give, but 10,000 *baht*—?"

As we knelt to pray, I couldn't help entertaining an almost smug feeling, surmising how God was going to answer our prayer.

Supervising students would never become just a routine job to me, but the days slipped into weeks and the weeks into months.

One evening Mother and I had finished eating when the screen door opened and Samruay walked into the apartment. Dropping to his knees by Mother's chair, Samruay stared at her ears. Looking up at me, Samruay spoke softly, a shade of awe in his voice, "Oh, grandma have long life; have long ears like the Buddha!"

I smiled, then impulsively asked, "Samruay, how come you don't bow your head when we pray to God at worship periods in the dormitory? Even if you don't believe, bowing your head shows respect, like taking off one's shoes when entering a Buddhist *wat*."

"Sometimes can; sometimes cannot," Samruay mumbled.

"What would you think of my respect for Thai temples if I sometimes removed my shoes and sometimes I didn't?"

Without warning Samruay burst into tears. "I want to die! Life so bad on compound!"

After much coaxing, Samruay confided he was being watched and told that he would be beaten up outside the compound if he in any way yielded to the Christian religion. He refused to divulge any names, a big sigh escaping his lips. He was hungry for normal family ties, but squeezed between two religions. I wondered how much longer Samruay could hold up.

Late fall brought Pastor Andrew Fearing to the compound for a Week of Spiritual Emphasis. After the first meeting *Khun* Vanna came back to the dormitory, her face aglow.

"*Mem kha*, no wonder you so strong for God. If I listen every week to *Adjohn* Fearing, I strong too!"

I nodded in agreement. At times our worship talks were delivered by well-meaning, but just-learning Thai ministerial interns recently off the rice paddies, their Bible stories at times garbled.

"*Khun* Vanna, how are the parents responding to the letter you sent out for donations to the building fund?" Secure in the knowledge we had already reached our goal and not having anything to do with the students' mail (all mail passed through Vanna's hands for censorship, as allowed in Thailand), I had completely forgotten to ask how the contributions were coming in.

"*Mem kha*, I wait for you to ask." Vanna's face beamed like a morning sunrise. "We almost reach 10,000 *baht*!"

"Really?" We would reach the $500 goal again? Was God trying to show me He was not miserly in His giving as I was, but extravagantly abundant? My smug assumption lay humbled in the dust as my heart began to fathom that dizzying promise—"All things are possible to him that believeth."

After a prayer of gratitude to God, Vanna turned

back to perusing the *Bangkok Post*, an English newspaper. Peering over her shoulder at a picture of His and Her Majesties of Thailand, I offhandedly remarked, "What a funny little pillbox hat the Queen is wearing."

"*Mem kha*!" Vanna's voice sounded strong, if not stern. "We *never* say anything against our king or queen!"

Figuratively, my mind sat up and took note of the Thais' strong loyalty to the royal pair. I knew that in talking to royalty or about royalty the Thai people use what amounts to a separate language, strange-sounding Thai words of reverence. And to appear in the presence of Their Majesties a person must be clothed in what is considered proper attire. As a Christian, my mind mused, was I showing as great respect for my God, Ruler of the universe, as the Thai people show for their earthly potentate? Moments like this made me aware that God had sent me to Thailand not only to teach, but also to learn.

Student Strike!

Leaving Mother with a few of the student nurses who were only too happy to occupy my place in an air-conditioned bedroom, Helen and I sought a respite from the compound routine on a weekend jaunt upcountry to Ubol. A blaring headline in the Bangkok English newspaper rudely interrupted our peaceful holiday.

"Helen! Look at that newspaper headline: STUDENT STRIKE AT MISSION HOSPITAL!"

We both made a grab for the paper, our hearts thumping as we read.

Helen summed up the details. "Several male students are revolting against the hospital's training school rules."

"They're claiming cruel treatment on the part of national leaders." I pointed to a paragraph. "Oh, *Khun* Vanna is their main target! She is strict, but she is also kind and so helpful to the students."

By the time Helen and I returned to BAH, we found a youthful rebellion blazing on the compound like a wind fanning a spark into brush fire. Even some of the Christian students became confused and entered the revolt.

Rules were for the purpose of orderliness and harmony, but, inspired perhaps by student revolts in other nearby countries, a few strong personalities felt that they, too, were being held down. Several teachers were sent to investigate other nursing schools in Bangkok. If too strong, the BAH rules would be amended.

The committee returned, their Thai chairman reporting, "Our school rules are far more lenient than those of Chulalongkorn or Sirirat Schools of Nursing." She hesitated, then smiling apologetically at the Americans present added, "One Thai director told us this was probably due to the *farang* influence in our hospital."

Students now filed by my open office door, stonily looking straight ahead, their usual smile or contagious "*Sawaddi kha, Mem*!" entombed in a heart churning with hostile emotions. My own heart smoldered at their unjust attitude to me. I longed for my controllable typewriter!

My motto came to my rescue: "Not to know any thing among you, save Jesus Christ and him crucified." I was an ambassadress for Christ! I would love the striking students back, biding my time until their vengeful spirits burned out.

Within the week students began slipping into my office, dropping to their knees, regretful tears spilling down their cheeks. They were but children in a world gone wrong; but love, the healing balm, had drawn them back. I, as well as the students, had learned a valuable lesson.

But in the turmoil, a chapter had been closed in the life of one student on the compound—Samruay, the former priest. Caught in the emotional upheaval and not looking beyond himself for more than human solutions, Samruay walked out of it all, a sad ending to his year at BAH. I regretted he had not accepted the help he could have found in Christianity. I could only pray that the seed sown would someday germinate.

A few weeks later the students forgot their grievances in looking forward to the yearly yuletide festivities on the compound. Lively carols resounded through the corridors with a wondrous Thai accent. The sweet spirit of Christmas descended, returning the compound to its usual serene and Christian atmosphere.

The end of May brought a flurry of monsoon rains as well as graduation preparations. The yearly senior banquet of the BAH training schools was held in one of the hotels in Bangkok. A special dessert—baked Alaska—rounded out the menu. The faculty member who brought the dessert noticed it was served with a crystal-clear sauce. Having no flavor, it neither added nor detracted from the cake. After the banquet she went to the kitchen to pick up her container. The cans of chemicals to keep the cake frozen were not there.

"Where are my cans of chemicals?" she asked the head waiter.

"Kem-i-cal?" The waiter looked bewildered.

"You know, keep cake cool with cold cans."

The waiter's face turned ashen as her words gradually registered in his mind. "Not sauce for cake?"

"Sauce?" the teacher's voice rose almost to a scream.

Not being able to read the English wording and thinking it was sauce, the kitchen staff had punctured the cans and poured the contents on the pieces of cake!

"We might all die!" The distraught teacher's words bounced off the kitchen walls. Several of the waiters, having poured a generous portion of the "sauce" over their pieces of leftover cake, stepped outside the hotel and began heaving.

The punctured cans were finally located and the warning on the label read, Not for consumption, but not harmful. Everyone breathed more easily again, and, fortunately, no one became ill from the supposed sauce. Nevertheless, the language barrier, often a comedy of errors, could have proved fatal to the senior classes at BAH as well as to the entire faculty.

I sat alone at the dean's desk, the wide-open windows letting in the quaint sound of Thai voices singing in the church. My year of supervising the dormitory almost over, I looked forward to the return of the furloughing dean, Esther Feltus. More than ever I held Aunt Esther in high esteem for her unruffled Christian spirit and tireless energy in guiding the students.

My months as acting dean had been a hard year for me, but rewarding too. Like a colorful changing kaleidoscope, frame after frame of relationships with students flickered through my mind.

The first frame formed the faces of "my girls." Vi, the unpredictable little Indian, graduated in June in a beautiful sari ceremony. Kim, beautiful but headstrong, came back from a vacation disgruntled with the world in general and with her dean in particular. I kept my distance as much as possible, considering I was her dean, praying that time would bring us together again.

The frame containing Chintara, dimples flashing, puzzled me. Still studying the Bible with others, she excused her reluctance to follow Christ all the way. She said she feared other students would say she would be doing this to get "in" with the missionaries.

I shuddered a bit at the frame of third-year student Prom, her belt tied in a noose around her neck, hanging from the shower-curtain rod in the dean's office bathroom! I could still hear the calm voice of her class sponsor saying, "Don't be frightened, Jeane," his finger pointing to Prom's feet planted firmly on the floor. This shattering experience occurred over a relatively minor misdemeanor! Girls, I discovered, were the same the world over, naughty as well as nice.

At the sound of a snapping twig, my kaleidoscope of images blurred. I glanced outside. No wind stirred the leaves of the trees. The evening grew more oppressive, even sinister. I shivered, feeling as though someone were watching me, but only darkness met my gaze. My eyes turned back to the paper work on my desk.

I had heard no one open the dormitory's front door, but a moment later I sensed someone standing in front of my desk. Looking up and seeing a man staring silently down at me, I let out a muffled cry. Samruay had come back!

"Samruay! I'm so glad to see you!" As I came around the desk, Samruay fell to his knees. "You don't need to kneel, Samruay. Please stand up."

Samruay arose and tears, more of those same old tears, filled his eyes. "Sorry I leave. Cannot stay."

"I know." In the midst of my concern, I noticed Samruay was beginning to pronounce his r's. "You have never given your heart to Jesus, Samruay."

"I Thai."

His reply brought to mind the Thai charms he once laid on my desk. "Jesus calls every person to follow Him, no matter what nationality."

Samruay changed the subject. "My mother come home?"

"No, Dr. Ethel is still on furlough in America."

"Oh, not like."

"Samruay, I went to see your five adopted mothers."

65

"Why?" His voice sounded hurt.

"I felt I owed them an explanation of your leaving."

"They very angry with me."

After Samruay left, a melancholy mood enveloped me. The former priest's days had been frustratingly disappointing at BAH. Similarly, Nara's seesaw experience in seeking Christ had ended in an attempted suicide. Now, working at another hospital, Nara sought freedom from the Christian way that, unaccepted, left her with a deep guilt complex.

It seemed that more of the bitter than the sweet of missionary life was reaching into my heart. A thought from *The Desire of Ages* came into my mind: "As the world's Redeemer, Christ was constantly confronted with apparent failure."—Page 678. But, my heart cried out, how could I let these dear Thai people go? Burying my head in my arms on the desk, I let the tears flow, washing away the question and bringing me the answer. My prayers could still reach out for their souls, but one thing I must never forget: I had only been commanded to sow the gospel seed; the harvest was in God's hands!

Rafting Down the Mae Ping

Yesterdays scribblings still finely etched in my heart, I found solace in the new day's tide of adventure. I'd been caught up in planning an exciting vacation—a raft trip down the Mae Ping River of northern Thailand. Not purely a vacation trip, it was to be a missionary venture as well. The doctors of BAH looked forward to going upcountry to do some clinical work, a change from the routine office clinics. I felt especially fortunate to be asked to go along.

Two years before, the Nelson family and I visited one of the many princes in Thailand to get information for taking the trip. After the Thai greeting, the prince clapped his hands, and a pretty, barefoot Thai girl appeared at the door. Dropping to the floor like a crumpling flower, she bowed low and glided over to the prince on her knees. After asking us what soft drink we preferred, the prince spoke rapidly to the girl, who silently backed out of the room, still on her knees. I felt as though the prince had drawn us far back into the pages of Siamese history.

That year our raft trip didn't materialize, for the chief rafter, as the men who pole-guide the rafts are called, was murdered. I began to wonder if I really wanted to go down a lonely river at the mercy of a gang of rough rafters! However, a new dam was being built near the village of Yanhee, and soon part of the river would become a great lake of backed-up water. Taking the raft trip down the Mae Ping was now or never.

In a small hired bus our raft group bumped along an oxcart trail to Bahn In for our rendezvous with five quaint, but lonely looking, newly constructed rafts.

"Ethel, are those our rafters?" I nodded my head toward a group of coarse-looking Thai men standing near the river's edge.

Ethel's eyes followed my head motion. "Ten men, right? Two for each raft. Guess they are."

Recalling their murdered chief, I felt a shiver run down my spine.

With four of us occupying one raft, there was just room enough for two sleeping bags one each side of the center pole. We tied our mosquito nets securely to the braces at the top of the raft hut and thus had a cozy boudoir where we could dress in a semblance of privacy.

The first morning, voices awakened me. Peeping out of the mosquito net, I saw the rafters lounging outside their bamboo bivouacs on the sandy beach, placidly eating their breakfast of rice. In the morning glow of a soon-rising sun, they didn't appear so formidable.

The rafters disappeared before we started eating. Shortly thereafter people began streaming out of the jungle behind the beach, all heading for our camp. There were men wearing baggy pants and women clad in dark colors and smoking homemade cigars. Grannies, bare to the waist, came with children, some only in shirts, some only in pants, and some in nothing. Many of the children, six years and older, were smoking! The missing rafters had been rounding up patients for our first clinic.

The clinic proved disastrous for a thumb and for my reputation. Dr. Roger came over with a fat brown baby needing a penicillin injection and, squeezing a hunk of buttock skin, told me to give the shot.

"I can't judge my aim, Dr. Roger, unless I hold the skin myself."

"Go ahead," he urged. "You can aim it all right."

I aimed it all right, but the thick needle went right through Roger's thumb, nail and all, and into the baby's buttock. Mortified, I started to withdraw the needle.

"No, Jeane!" the doctor's voice stopped me. "Go ahead and give the shot through my thumb. No need to stick the baby twice."

The people gladly received the Thai-language literature, medical and spiritual, handed out to them after the clinic. Prakaiwan, a lab student, taught the Thai children to sing "*Ha Phra Jesu*." ("Come to Jesus") to the tune of "Clementine." As our rafts drifted away into the current, we could hear the Thai children in their sweet, lilting voices singing the song they'd just learned.

For the next ten days clinics became a daily ritual after breakfast and lunch. However, in the evenings our fleet of rafts snuggled up to a secluded beach, away from the curious public. The rafters, sitting on the sand by their hastily erected bivouacs, smoked home-made, pint-sized cigars and contentedly watched us having evening worship. Somjean, another lab student, translated the talks into Thai for the benefit of the nearby rafters. Prakaiwan had confided, "Rafters tell me in all trips down river, some fifty, they never meet people like us!"

No phones! No doorbells! No schedules! Just a lazy drifting down our ribbon waterway that meandered through plains and twisted like a snake around small hills and finally craggy mountains. I whiled away the time looking through my binoculars at fabulous birds, fleet-footed deer, and tree-hopping monkeys. Sometimes I practiced my Thai on Dep, the rafter on my end of the raft. We'd broken through the prejudice of the rafters. Now they came regularly to our evening worship, sitting in the background puffing on their cigars, singing "*Jah Sadit Glop Mah*" ("Jesus Is Coming Again"). And to think I was once afraid of them!

On Sabbath the rafters, who apparently couldn't understand our stopping in one spot for a whole day, watched our activities intently. As we watched theirs, for the rafters had been staying apart from us, we asked Prakaiwan to find out what we had done to offend them.

Prakaiwan returned, a sly grin on her face. "We not offend. They not understand people like us. We not smoke, drink, or play cards, just wash clothes all the time and bring medicine to Thai people." Pointing to the rafters' emergency bamboo clothesline, she ended, "Afraid they smell and offend us, so wash clothes and selves!" The clean-up job produced a startling effect—the rafters had the appearance of a new crew!

A few days after this the rafters began talking excitedly among themselves. Somjean translated, "Current leaving river! Soon too deep for rafters' fifteen-foot poles to touch bottom. Need boat to pull us in!"

"A boat!" I echoed. "Somjean, we haven't seen a boat for days!"

It was noontime. We ate a hurried lunch, ending with the oft-repeated cookie dessert. (Would I ever relish a cookie again?) Suddenly our ears picked up a put-put sound. A motorboat? We had prayed for one only moments before, and now, around the bend of the river it came, but going in the wrong direction! However, the affable Thai owner agreed to turn around and pull us to the dam. With our rafts tied together like a long train, shabby-looking from use, we started off.

About the middle of the afternoon the motorboat suddenly coughed, sputtered, and stopped in the middle of the river now metamorphosed into a great lake. We were marooned above who-knows-how-many feet of water!

After dusk, Dep and Gaow, our two rafters, and I chatted spasmodically—my Thai often failing. Orion, with its brilliant stars, scintillated above us like a costly brooch in the now-velvety night sky.

In my choppy Thai I tried to explain, "Jesus will return through the stars to take back to heaven those who believe in Him." The two rafters, awed at their first sight of stars magnified through binoculars, exclaimed, "*Mem, bai duey* [Go too]!"

The date dawned on me—December 17, my second anniversary in Thailand—and here I was, stranded on a trainlike raft of bamboo, communicating with upcountry Thai people about Jesus!

Just then the motor of the boat began to sputter and cough, followed by the beautiful put-put sound. Slowly we crept along, a lantern throwing eerie light in the murky water a few feet ahead to keep us from running into submerged treetops and upsetting our chain of rafts. We soon docked at a small mountaintop, our rafts jutting out from the island like a dilapidated pier.

Next morning, towed over a mirror-smooth lake encircled by mountaintop islands, we glided past tips of roofs, *wats*, and tall coconut trees jutting out of the inundating waters. Without a sign of violence, it held a beauty all its own. And then our odyssey down the

71

Mae Ping abruptly ended at the partially completed massive dam.

Once again our souls had been washed in God's magnificent nature. But best of all, we'd blended our vacation with witnessing for Jesus. Not only had we helped Thai people's physical needs, but we'd reached into the hearts of our rafters, as well as sprinkled the wonderful gospel story deep in the heart of Thailand!

Eyhui, a Thai Nightingale

While eating dinner one Sabbath with a group of students, I developed a throbbing headache that refused to go away.

"Girls, do you mind if I go and lie down?"

I retired to the bedroom, but not to sleep. By evening my temperature had risen. For the next five days, dengue fever, caused by a virus carried by mosquitoes, raged within my body. Stabbing pains in my head made my eyes feel as if they were springing back and forth yo-yo fashion. Red spots broke out on my body, and every bone ached. Now I knew why someone dubbed the illness "breakbone fever"!

As I lay in my bed of pain that first day, cool hands gently touched my brow. "*Mem kha!*" Soft and bell-like, the Thai voice reached into my consciousness. I opened my eyes in the shade-drawn room and saw the form of a nurse, fine boned in features, kneeling by my side.

"I pray for you," she said. Her simply spoken empathy resounded in her words of prayer.

"Thank you, Eyhui."

"*Mem kha*, no need to talk. I just sit here on the rug beside you."

Eyhui, already a graduate nurse when I came to

Bangkok, had a naturally tender spirit that endeared her to the patients of BAH. And fellow employees, as well as students, knew where to go on the hospital compound for a sympathetic listening ear. Now, sitting quietly by my bed of pain, this rare quality of love and compassion radiated into my own life as Eyhui gently laid a cool cloth on my burning brow.

There was no cure for the fever, just aspirin, and that didn't begin to alleviate the sharp head pains and aching body. In my extreme misery even God seemed far away and out of reach. But He hadn't forsaken me.

Word of my illness spread around the compound. White-gowned shapes and broken-English voices kept coming to my bedside. The feared "breakbone fever" drew me into even closer contact with the people I loved and brought into my life a new revelation—the TLC (tender loving care) of the wonderful Oriental students and nurses!

As the fever abated somewhat, Eyhui sat near my bed chatting about her life, trying to get my mind off my still-aching body.

"My cousin take nursing at BAH, so I apply, too, and am accepted. Cousin warn me to ignore Christian teaching. I agree, as did my parents, that I would not let it affect me. But is strange. I feel drawn to the Bible classes. To get away from this attraction my mind try to think up hard questions to put Bible teacher on the spot. Instead, I get deeper and deeper into Christianity, understand it more and more.

"*Mem kha*, the Christian's message worm its way into my heart!" Remembering, Eyhui's eyes filled with tears. "I kept telling myself, 'I will not accept! I hate it! I hate it!' But you know what? One Sabbath afternoon while taking a nap, I dream Christ come! It so real. I wake up, and my clothes all wet from sweat. Falling

74

on my knees I cried, 'Lord, thank You. Still time to be a Christian!' I could not fight it any longer." Wonder crept into Eyhui's voice. "I knew I loved the Christian's Jesus! But, besides my parents, another person did not want me to become a Christian—my boyfriend, who love me very much."

Eyhui went on to tell how she went to see the hospital church pastor, and in her forward way said, "I want to be baptized this next Sabbath!"

Knowing how coldly, sometimes even antagonistically, Eyhui had always responded to personal appeals, the pastor cautioned, "I believe it would be better for you to wait and study more."

Eyhui went on to plead her case. "Pastor, I am fourth-year student and have much Bible study. I understand. But if I not baptize immediately, I am afraid I listen to boyfriend and never come in." Eyhui then related to the pastor her dream.

After the pastor's consent, Eyhui went home to see her boyfriend with the direct announcement, "I will become Christian next Sabbath!"

Startled by her open declaration, he cried out, "Eyhui, don't you love me anymore?"

"I do love you, and I know you love me." Realizing that her words would sever a relationship that had grown very dear, her voice dropped to a mere whisper, "But I know Christ loves me more!"

Begging her to reconsider, her boyfriend finally threw himself on his knees and put his arms around her ankles.

"*Mem kha*," Eyhui's voice trembled, "in Thailand this action show deep respect for woman and shred my heart. But I remember, I baptize next Sabbath!" Tears streamed even more heavily down Eyhui's cheeks.

"Did you see your boyfriend any more?"

"Only a few times." Eyhui went on to tell how he tried to dissuade her and she, in turn, tried to persuade him to study the Bible. But he remained as adamant as she—a heartbreaking deadlock!

My bout of fever finally left. The red spots cleared up. And dengue fever was only a bad memory, except for the loving care of the Oriental Nightingales. Now I knew from experience the depth of the Thai axiom: A mosquito is more to be feared than a tiger!

November brought the scintillating Thai festival of *Loy Krathong*. As dusk faded into a full-moon night, I drove a VW busload of students to watch the flower-bedecked *krathongs*. These were banana-leaf boats carrying offerings of food, betel nut, and a coin or two. Pious people in an act of merit would cast their banana-leaf boats upon the rivers and ponds! The owners would offer a prayer to the Mother of Waters, asking forgiveness for polluting her bountiful streams, and then *loy*—float their atonement away.

The mass piety of the loving Thai people around me and the hundreds of thousands of *krathongs*, their tiny tapers glittering in the water, pulled at my heartstrings. In Buddhism, "man is as he has made himself"; the individual has to strive to be pure of heart and deed for his own salvation.

Tired more in spirit than in body, I drove the students back to the compound. I had just walked into my apartment when Helen called from the front door.

"Jeane, have you seen the *Bangkok Post* today?"

"No. Come on in!"

"You missed a very important item!"

"Helen, news is so ephemeral; tomorrow it won't be important anymore."

"This will!" Helen pointed to a small item in the newspaper.

Curious, I leaned over and read aloud. "The speeches for the Bangkok Toastmistress Club this week will be given by . . . " My eyes skipped over the names, knowing that one would be mine, and dropped to the last line. "This week's toastmistresses will be participating in a speech contest." Turning to Helen I gasped, "They've *got* to be kidding!"

"Afraid not," Helen sympathized.

"But when I scheduled my speech no one told me it was a contest," I fretted. "And, Helen, here it is only three days away, and I'm working on a talk on birds. Birds! I can't begin to compete against Countess Valinski of Australia and the Swiss ambassador's wife! Why, those sophisticated women will make my birds look like—like feather dusters!"

Fine Feathered Friends of Khao Yai

Helen, who was a member of the Bangkok Toastmistress Club when I came to Thailand, convinced me, after returning from America where I had been called to give talks in schools, churches, and clubs, that I should join the speech club to improve my public speaking. When signing up for my fourth speech, a talk requiring objects or illustrations, my fine feathered friends of Khao Yai, which means "Big Mountain," seemed a natural subject. I could show bird pictures while talking.

Now, as Helen walked briskly up the steps to the room where the Toastmistress meeting was held, I found myself lagging behind.

Turning around, Helen laughed, "Jeane, quit dragging your heels. It's just a talk!"

"Probably my last one too!" I predicted, gloom saturating me.

On entering the room, I rested my eyes momentarily on one group of women including Countess Valinski, self-confident and strong in personality. She brandished the usual smoldering cigarette in an ostentatious holder. I cringed mentally, remembering that she, too, had a speech in today's contest.

The president called the meeting to order. After a

discussion of old and new business, she produced the prize for the winning contestant—a silver ashtray engraved with the words Toastmistress Speech Winner. A perfect gift, my mind mused, for Countess Valinski!

I couldn't help observe, almost enviously, with what ease the two speeches before mine were given. With a last inaudible appeal to my Friend in heaven, "You know I don't want the ashtray, Jesus, but please keep me from falling flat on my face." I arose and took my place behind the rostrum.

My legs felt as though they were turning to jelly as my eyes took in the cosmopolitan club members before me, women from the upper echelon of society in Thailand and around the world—Khunjing Sommook, of high breeding; Mom Kop Kaew, a minor wife of the grandson of King Chulalongkorn; a Thai princess; and ambassadors' wives. With my unruly heart beating like a tom-tom, I announced my talk, "Feathered Friends of Khao Yai."

After describing Khao Yai, a mountain retreat where the jungle emitted a great variety of strange noises, from marauding monkeys to screeching, but exotic, birds, I told the following experience:

From a tree near our cabin, Dr. Ethel Nelson, my birding friend, and I heard a hollow sound, like a woodpecker. Running outside, we barely sighted a beautiful golden-backed bird, when it flew just inside the nearby jungle. We had been warned by the Thai rangers of Khao Yai not to venture inside the jungle alone, as a tiger had been spotted prowling in the area. But, hoping for a better look at the bird, we unthinkingly ran into the jungle. As I got my binoculars adjusted on the bird, my ears picked up a panting sound coming through the jungle toward us.

"Ethel!" My voice dropped to a bare whisper. "I can't lower my binocs. I'll lose the bird. What's that breathing sound?"

"Don't know," came my friend's clipped reply. "But where's the bird? Oh, I just sighted it!"

The panting noise steadily grew closer. My heart began to pound. But, in true ornithology fashion, I refused to take my binoculars off the bird, and quietly breathed, "Oooh, the head is gorgeous, a red—" I didn't finish my sentence, for the panting noise seemed to be almost upon us! We both ducked to protect ourselves just as the sound passed *over* our heads! Running out of the jungle, we saw a flock of the queerest and most extraordinary birds flying in formation like a ballet troupe just above the treetops. Their wing beats, a rhythmic one, two, three, and then a glide, made a panting sound like the heavy breathing of a tiger. It was my first look at the huge, grotesque hornbills.

I had caught my sophisticated audience's attention, and knowing my subjects personally—God's feathered creatures in nature—I began to talk freely about them, almost at ease. The previously bored aura in the room began to break down, replaced by a warm, friendly atmosphere.

After describing several more exotic birds to my now-captivated audience, I closed my speech by giving God the glory for creating the beauty of color and song in nature for mankind's enjoyment and reassurance, knowing that not even a drab little sparrow in Bangkok falls but what the great Master Creator Himself is cognizant!

As always, God sustained me, and then blessed me far beyond my greatest expectations—I won the speech contest! Clutching the silver ashtray, later to be converted into a catchall for my dresser, I received the congratulations of the toastmistresses as if in a dream. Most thrilling of all, cultured Thai women captured a glimpse of beauty, previously unknown, among God's feathered creatures in their own country!

My prediction of the speech being my last came true, but, happily, not as I expected. On our way home, Helen suggested we start our own toastmistress club on the compound, helping the teachers of the nursing school and hospital employees to improve their English so they might understand the English-speaking patients better. I fell in with the plan, and we never returned to the more elite group in Bangkok.

"Grandma"

The day dawned bright and sunny. I had no warning that it would be any different from any other working day. Early showers the month before had brought a delicious crop of mangoes, and Mother and I breakfasted on some luscious *nam dok mai* (nectar of the flowers), sweet and syrupy.

As we ate we talked on our favorite subject, the spiritual atmosphere at BAH, which was growing stronger. The first domestic helpers on the compound had recently been baptized. The church membership had risen to over one thousand. Considering the more than 30 million people in the land, this wasn't even a drop in the bucket. However, where before only ten or twelve people accepted Christ each year, now almost a hundred were coming in!

Mother suddenly changed the subject. "Jeane, the monsoons are coming soon."

I looked up. "Oh, no, Grandma." I used the affectionate name the nationals had given Mother. "It is only the middle of April."

"They are coming early this year," Mother insisted. "I feel it in my bones. Mark my words; it will soon start raining!"

As I left for the office, I cautioned our helper to

watch Mother carefully as she was having some strange black-out spells. At noon the doctor checked Mother and found her heart sounding strong and in good rhythm. I felt better.

Eyhui was to eat lunch with us, so I hurried over to the hospital to leave a prescription to be filled at the pharmacy. When I returned, the dining room was still empty. I went to the bedroom, but stopped short at the door. Dr. Ethel and another missionary doctor stood at the bedside, bending over Mother.

Hearing my approach, Dr. Ethel looked up and walked over to me. She placed her arm tenderly around me. "Jeane, Grandma's gone!"

Gone? I couldn't believe it! I simply couldn't grasp the fact that Mother's sojourn on this earth had abruptly come to an end. *She was gone!*

"Jeane," Helen's voice came through the blackness that surrounded me. "Why don't you come into the living room and sit down awhile. Dr. Ethel and I will take care of things for you."

I sat down in a chair near the front door as Eyhui came from the kitchen. Falling on her knees by my chair, Eyhui exclaimed, "*Mem kha*, I feel so badly about Grandma!" Big tears rolled down her cheeks. With my sorrow so sudden, I'd forgotten we'd invited Eyhui to lunch.

I felt unprepared for the traumatic experience I'd been plunged into, its tentacles deep and enveloping. For a moment I longed to be alone with my grief and let myself sink into its clutches. And yet, knowing Eyhui was still a child in the ways of the Lord, a stronger force compelled me to assuage her sorrow.

"Eyhui, if faithful, we'll see Grandma again at the first resurrection," I murmured. The words sounded hollow to my own ears, for my heart sorrowed on.

The news spread around the compound. People began streaming into the apartment from every department in the hospital—nurses, students, office workers, even maintenance men. First, they went into the bedroom to see their friend Grandma for the last time, it being the custom in Thailand not to open the casket at a funeral, but to put a large picture of the deceased on top of it. Then they came to kneel by my chair, many sobbing forlornly. Smiling feebly through tears trickling down my cheeks like a never-ending fountain, I tried to assure them of Grandma's love for Jesus and that "if faithful, we will see her again at the first resurrection." The words, repeated over and over and over, at last ignited a spark in my grief-stricken heart and flamed into a bright hope—Mother's faith in Jesus, firm to the end, would bring her back to life at the resurrection morning!

Because of the poor condition of the hospital morgue and the primitive type of embalming available in Bangkok, it was decided to have the funeral that afternoon. All was in readiness, even to a beautiful steel-gray casket left by an American embassy funeral and Dr. Ethel's foresight in having it stored away in the godown.

Four o'clock came. Soft breezes, cooled by an early-afternoon storm, wafted across the congregation. Mother's predicted monsoon had come and gone.

"My girl" Kim, our relationship long mended, came over to stay a few days with me, bringing youthful cheerfulness into the apartment. We shared the cards, letters, and telegrams that came flooding in, including a note from Gumjorn, a ministerial intern who now pastored a church on the island of Phuket.

I first met Gumjorn when Helen inveigled me to join choir rehearsals my second day in Thailand. Introductions came at me from all sides with Thai names so long and foreign sounding, they went in one ear and out the other—until I met Gumjorn.

"If you can't remember the name Gumjorn, Jeane, just think of gumdrop!" Helen suggested. Everybody laughed, including Gumjorn.

The prop stuck, but even without it I would have remembered, for Gumjorn himself held my attention— an Oriental version of the younger of my two brothers! And the similarity went one step farther, a rich singing voice. Gumjorn sang from a deep personal feeling of his need of Christ that charmed the hearts of his hearers. With his many talents, Gumjorn gave promise of doing great things for the work of God in Thailand. I learned, however, that he suffered from a tricky heart that sometimes beat out of rhythm. Once he had almost died from this malady.

Looking at Gumjorn's Oriental way of ending his note of sympathy brought a smile to my lips; it was innocently signed, "Many loves."

After Kim went back to the dormitory, I invited Eyhui over for lunch, a rain check on the one she had missed. While eating, we heard wooden getas slowly clopping up the walk—Mrs. Quah, supervisor of the hospital laundry department.

"Come in!" I called, but since she didn't enter, I went to the door.

"Cannot stay, but I share something to show how much I miss seeing Grandma sitting out here on the porch in her chair. Grandma always had a smile on her face and strong faith in her voice. The missionaries taught us how to live, but Grandma taught us how to die!" Mrs. Quah handed me a bunch of flowers, then shuffled away, wiping her eyes.

In her seventies, Mrs. Quah had already outlived the

normal span of life in the Orient. Her words of tribute made me realize that Mother's few years in Thailand had been fragrant with unobtrusive, but fruit-bearing missionary zeal.

Upon my return to the table, Eyhui spoke, "*Mem kha*, you have given me my second lesson in being a Christian."

"Second?"

"Yes! When you come, I ask Mrs. Sprengel why you not married. When she told me, I have first lesson. If you can make it through life by losing a husband after accepting Jesus, I can give up just a boyfriend!"

"Oh, Eyhui, that is why you asked me some time ago how I can live the Christian life?"

"Yes. You tell me it is day-by-day experience and God always help. Then I decide to try harder. I watch your life. The day Grandma die, I see with my own eyes you comfort people instead of being comforted, even smile with running down tears." Eyhui shook her head. "This, I tell myself, is way Christian should act. I learn second lesson."

After Eyhui left, I realized only too well my shortcomings as a Christian example and how little I deserved the confidence she placed in me. I trembled at the thought of the many eyes on the compound, Christian and Buddhist, watching, scrutinizing, the life of the missionary!

Siriporn: Trial by Fire

I, who had always resisted change, was beginning to detect that missionary life entailed being able to accept constant change, even at a moment's notice.

First, Kim graduated and due to immigration problems, left Bangkok practically overnight to work in Penang.

Next, a housing shortage developed on the BAH compound, and the committee assigned a new single missionary to a makeshift apartment. She, naturally, was unhappy, but the medical director didn't know how to solve the dilemma. I offered to let her room with me, not really wanting to, but hoping for a solution. (Would my selfish heart ever spontaneously give of itself to others!) She moved in, but this created a problem of a different kind. In our one-bedroom apartment, with my habit of being early to bed and hers late, we were utterly incompatible.

We lived together a week, our nerves becoming ragged from our differing temperaments. I really didn't want to leave my pleasant abode, but couldn't see any other alternative. Wondering if I would be sorry later, I asked permission to move into the vacated apartment in spite of its drawbacks.

Soon after my move, the hospital, seeking to rid the

compound of an over-running population of rats, put out poison, but forgot to tell the residents about it. Roaming pets, including my huge beautifully-marked Siamese cat, imbibed the poison and soon developed the fatal symptoms.

My Bangkok world seemed to be turning flip-flops!

"Malee," I sympathized with my new Christian helper, crying quietly, "I too will miss our furry friend. But if I cry, it's going to be over people right here on this compound who refuse to accept Jesus!"

My strong words surprised even me but bolstered my own flagging spirits, already depressed by my housing problems. The monsoons, inundating the grounds with floodwater, backed up the toilet so that it didn't flush. And to top things off, the past Sabbath as I stepped out the kitchen door, a huge rat jumped onto my leg!

If the apartment continued at times to agitate my finer senses, the blessing that came with it far outweighed the inconveniences. Hudson Taylor, an old-time missionary to China, once stated, "You can't tell them what you sacrificed, you must *show* them!" He practiced this philosophy by living on the level of the Oriental people around him. I knew my spirit had not been of such a fine sacrificial flavor, for expediency had led me to make the move. However, God was allowing His reluctant servant to reap a rich benefit: acceptance by the nationals! And in this, I felt I had reached a cherished goal every missionary desires.

The spiritual work in Thailand progressed slowly; sometimes one even suspicioned it might be sliding backward! And then came a bit of harvest—an ordination service of three mission workers, Gumjorn being one of them, after working twelve years as a ministerial intern.

And on its heels came a Sabbath-vesper baptism, the largest ever held on the hospital compound. It included many workers from the various departments of the hospital. And to me, having studied with one of the candidates, student nurse Siriporn, the baptism came as a sweet bonus from God.

After my first week as acting dean at the student nurses' dormitory, I had asked Vanna, "Who is the student called Siriporn Tan?"

"First-year student from island of Phuket."

"Every night in study hall, *Khun* Vanna, I see her reading a devotional book before studying."

"She is Christian, but not our church." Vanna explained.

Becoming friends with Siriporn had led to Bible studies. At a recent Week of Spiritual Emphasis, Siriporn requested baptism. She would be the first student of another Protestant faith at BAH to accept additional light from the Bible. Knowing her former pastor would be making a trip from Phuket to Bangkok, I cautioned Siriporn to be sure to talk with him about her decision. I was disappointed, however, to learn that Siriporn had failed to tell him about her contemplated baptism. The Oriental shyness in facing a problem head on had again triumphed.

Word about the baptism reached Phuket by telegram. The following Tuesday Siriporn heard that her former pastor was returning to Bangkok on Wednesday to see her!

The pastor arrived at ten o'clock, and Siriporn and he went into the sitting room to talk. At noon I called the dean's office and was told they were still talking. I called again at two and at five and was given the same message: They were *still* talking! At six o'clock my phone jangled, and I jumped to answer it.

"Jeane, this is Helen. Would you mind coming over to the dormitory? Siriporn needs you."

"Has the pastor left?"

"Yes. That poor girl hasn't had food or drink since morning!"

Dressed to go out to dinner with friends, I dashed over to the dormitory.

"Siriporn, is there anything I can do to help you?"

Siriporn nodded her head. "Yes, may I go home with you?"

The unexpected request caused me to hesitate. My evening was planned. Looking down at Siriporn sitting so forlornly on the hard dormitory bed, her eyes red and swollen from crying, I knew where my missionary duty lay.

"Siriporn, you run along and take a quick shower. Then come over to the apartment. All right?"

After bathing, Siriporn looked refreshed and could feebly smile again: The battle had been won. The pastor had begged, pleaded, and sobbed for her to come back to his church. They talked, they prayed, they cried for seven and one-half hours!

"*Mem kha*, first time I join Christian faith in Phuket, is easy, but this time, oh, so hard! My former pastor is like a father to me, and I have hurt him very much. How I regret not taking your advice and telling him I plan to baptize. He heard rumors and asked, but I not answer him."

Through the ordeal Siriporn remained adamant about her decision. However, she agreed that when she came to Phuket she would be willing to talk over her newfound faith with the church. "Then," she stated, "you must show me from the Bible where I am wrong. If you can, I will reject this new faith and come back."

Siriporn's trial had come fast and fiery, her new faith branded a "heretic" religion. Nevertheless, Siriporn was not sorry she'd accepted the truths of the Bible. In fact they had become clearer and dearer than ever before!

Siriporn left and I started preparing for bed, when the phone rang. A military patient, to be evacuated early in the morning, needed a medical report ready to go with him.

Weary and anxious to get back home, I finished the three-page physical résumé and took the letter to the doctor's office to be signed.

The doctor reached for the report and then surprised me by saying, "Sit down, Jeane; I'd like to talk with you a little." Rather abruptly he queried, "You seem to like missionary life out here, don't you?"

I looked up, wondering just what the doctor was getting at. "Yes, I do."

His unreadable eyes studied me for a moment. When he spoke, a hint of incredulity crept into his voice. "You're here alone. You live in one of the worst housing situations on the compound. And in spite of it all, you're happy? Why do you like it here so well?"

I shrugged my shoulders. "I just do." Then, knowing some of the doctor's problems in adjusting to the compound, I decided to bare my inner thoughts, even though I had no planned answer to his pointed question.

"Before coming to Bangkok I took the motto 'not to know any thing among you, save Jesus Christ, and him crucified.' I knew I was basically selfish, but until I tried to live up to my motto, I didn't realize how ignoble I really was. I soon found I wasn't nearly as giving or generous as I imagined myself to be. Springing up were unexpected depths of selfishness, self-centered-

91

ness, in my nature. God began to show this to me by putting me into situations not of my own choosing or liking!" I paused, but the doctor said nothing. "Living up to my motto yielded flexibility, which seems to me to be the golden quality one needs to stay happy in the mission field."

Had my testimony helped resolve the doctor's problem? I didn't know, for again he said nothing, and his face remained unscrutible. He did, however, bid me a pleasant good night.

Home Leave

Four years had slipped by. It was furlough time—a whole year—and I was going home! Then the painful thought stabbed me, With Mother gone there was no home!

Deliberately I relegated the intruding thought to the back of my mind, knowing from experience that God would help me cope with the future as He had in the past. With forced gusto I began to tackle a home-leave itinerary—a relaxing week on a houseboat in Kashmir and, hopefully, an exciting two-week safari in East Africa.

My nomadic roving eventually led me to the picturesque Scandinavian countries. Then, tired of wandering, I again found myself basking in eager anticipation of reaching homeland soil. Peering through a porthole of the jet as it lost altitude, I watched the Los Angeles metropolis come into view below, clear and smogless.

It was pleasant to be in America. Nonetheless, I missed the noisy, overcrowded hospital compound. I watched the mailbox for blue aerogrammes like a hawk hovering over a field for prey. When a letter arrived from Helen, I curled up in a comfortable chair to read and relish every word. It seemed odd that the message was a carbon copy addressed to twelve people—missionaries living upcountry in Thailand and those on home leave.

My eyes skimmed over the first sentence—"Our hearts are heavy today—Gumjorn died last night!" Oh, no! my heart cried out. Through blurring vision I read the details of vainly trying to revive Gumjorn from heart failure by open-heart massage. The letter continued, "Gumjorn was only thirty-three and an ordained minister in a country that has only three. Now one is gone." The typewritten words disappeared completely as a watery veil streamed down my face. The enemy had struck a vital blow to the work in Thailand. And my heart ached in empathy to the quiet nurse-wife, now left with two school-age children.

Strong winds and cold rains lashed the coastline of California, chilling my Thai-baked bones. With a forecast of more inclement weather to come, I decided to move on to Hawaii for a couple of months, where it would be warmer. The remainder of my furlough I would spend meandering back to Thailand through the captivating Orient, reaching Bangkok by early summer.

But the best laid plans of mice and men. . . . While in Hawaii, I received a cablegram message from Southeast Asia Union asking if I would be willing to cut short my furlough and come to Singapore to help out a few months in the accounting office while workers attended meetings at the General Conference headquarters in Washington, D.C. I couldn't believe they would ask me, who couldn't keep my own bank account straight, to handle the accounts of the union involving five countries! But they did.

A Secret Caroling Agenda

Six months and my Singapore stint of accounting lay behind me. I had accepted the dreaded assignment with misgivings, but again I found God's appointments brought blessings—this time unforgettable missionary friendships, plus a greater respect for accountants!

Sensing my anxiety to return to the Thai people, the Singapore missionaries chided me about not appreciating the quiet union compound. Even I couldn't quite understand the cord of love that bound me to the sunbaked, overly crowded BAH compound.

It was good to be back in Thailand. It was home. Even the sturdy boughs of the parasol-like rain trees, almost brushing the louvered windows of my newly appointed, second-story abode in the hospital compound, reached out as if in welcome!

Cooling winds from the north stirred up emotions for the approaching Christmas season. I dragged out the holiday decorations, stringing tiny colored lights around a hanging lamp. At night their distorted reflections in the louvered windows nearby cast an array of shimmering rainbows around the living-room walls.

When I finished decorating, Wan Di swept up the debris in the room and carried the empty boxes to the bedroom for storing. The Sprengel family had left

Thailand permanently, and I found it consoling to have Wan Di working for me. Practicing my first Thai phrases on Wan Di in the Sprengel's kitchen, she had danced around on her bare feet, giggling, too shy to correct my jumbled Thai. Now her presence brought rays of Thai sunshine into the apartment.

Heavy Christmas-Eve traffic rumbled by on the two busy streets outside the compound. An unusual calm reigned inside, many missionaries and students having gone on the traditional choir-caroling appointments at embassies and hotels in Bangkok.

Reveling in an evening to myself, I picked up my Bible and, curling up on the sofa, began leafing through it. Barely deciphering the words in the glimmering Christmas lights, my eyes lingered on a familiar clause—"I will cause thee to ride upon the high places of the earth." Isaiah 58:14. The provocative words flooded me with memories of past Christmas Eves in Thailand when, as a member of the choir, our caroling appointments brought us into contact with the elite of the land. One appointment shone out above the others—a never-to-be-forgotten memory.

I had joined the gala choir group congregating at the back of the hospital to go caroling, the *farangs* (foreigners) talking a garbled Thai, and the Thais, a broken English. Helen, director of the choir at that time, for weeks had tantalized the members into well-attended rehearsals by hints of a special caroling appointment only for the "regulars."

As the choir members milled around in new white robes with reversible red and gold collars, she made known her secret agenda.

"Choir members, tonight we have an hour-long televised appointment at the residence of the Prime Minister of Thailand!" A hush fell over the group, the announcement being far more stupendous than any of us had imagined.

Arriving at the large government mansion, we paraded in rank and file to a picturesque miniature amphitheater formed by white pillars and tall leafy trees with lush green vines winding up their trunks. Our white robes, with the red satin collars out for Christmas, gave a festive air to the sylvan backdrop.

We began to sing under the close scrutiny of the TV cameras. The door of the palatial house opened, and the Prime Minister and his wife came out and sat down before us in white wrought-iron garden seats. With the last rays of the sun flickering through the shadowy trees and songbirds adding their lilting notes, we sang our repertoire of carols exalting the birth of Jesus, not only to an attentive Buddhist Prime Minister and his wife, but also to a vast TV audience of Thailand.

Next came the surprise of the evening—a garden buffet supper!

I leaned over toward Helen standing near me. "You didn't tell us this appointment included supper! And one of pizza at that!"

"No one told me, either!" Helen retorted as we both reached for a piece of the scrumptious-looking pizza and bit in.

I recovered first. "Whew! *Phet mak* [Very hot]! This pizza is topped with a peppery Thai sauce!"

Helen laughed, nodding in agreement.

In a country of perpetual perspiration, the paradoxical Thais are famous for their hot curries and sauces made from fiery peppers and spices. Those not used to it weep at a mere taste of the concoction that burns from the mouth down to the stomach, no amount of ice water alleviating it!

The Prime Minister circulated among us as we ate the tangy Thai pizza, the nationals relishing the *phet* (hot) flavor, the missionaries politely trying to make a small piece last as long as possible. As we got ready to leave, a Thai-version Santa Claus handed out diarylike booklets and hard candy. But my thoughts at the moment were on the privilege of presenting in song the message of Christ to the top government man of a Buddhist nation and his people.

With the yuletide lights shedding their hypnotic glow around me, I must have dozed off. Was I dreaming of hearing childish Thai voices singing carols? I jumped up from the sofa and looked out the window. In the grassy circle outside, Thai students, Buddhist and Christian, sang the old familiar carols with a charming Thai accent. As my eyes adjusted to the dimness below, I could see, standing in the midst of the students like a delicate flower, Mrs. Quah, singing with all her small might! Soon came the words, "We wish you a merry Christmas," as only the Thais can sing them, gradually fading into the distance, mingling with the clopping of wooden getas.

Mrs. Quah and the King of Siam

Monster kites, some six feet tall, careened wildly in the blue sky, while stiff March winds battered them to and fro like heaving waves berserk in a tropical storm. Avid kite flyers, the Thai people were holding their yearly Kite Flying Contest, a national sport, at the Pramane Grounds near the Emerald Buddha Temple.

From the roof of the hospital I watched the colorful display of kites sporting grotesquely in the air. The "male" kite, called the *chula*, soared back and forth, trying to encircle the string of the smaller *pukpao* "female" kite. The "female" kite, which had sharp glass attached to its string, tried, in turn, to cut down the approaching "male" kite.

Reluctantly I turned away from the merry Thai sport and started down the steps to my first-floor office. Now converted into a secretarial pool, our office was the recipient of a constant stream of activity flowing in from all the medical departments of the hospital. Two Filipino secretaries, prodigious workers, helped keep the medical reports up to date. Also, Lydia, in the record office, was still doing more than her share. We looked forward to several national girls, now taking a secretarial-science course in the Philippines, returning to BAH in a few years.

Five-thirty that evening, tired but with a satisfied feeling of a job well done by the secretaries, I closed the office door and went home. I ate the Thai fruit Wan Di had left for my supper, relishing each bite.

"Anyone home?" Mrs. Quah's voice floated up to me from the downstairs door.

"Do come up!" I called back.

Puffing slightly from the steep ascent, Mrs. Quah waved a sheaf of paper in her hand. "I hope I'm not rushing your eating, but I need some advice."

"You aren't," I assured her. "Make yourself comfortable while I take the dishes to the kitchen." Returning, I inquired, "What's the problem?"

"It's almost impossible to get the information the office wants on my laundry workers. For one thing, most of them don't know the year they were born. As to their children, they only know they were born in the year of the rabbit, the pig, and so on." A stickler for doing a job well, Mrs. Quah laid the papers down on the couch in frustration.

"Don't worry," I sympathized, picking them up. "In the morning I'll talk to the medical director about it for you." Laying the papers on the table, I asked, "Can you visit awhile? I've always wanted to hear your story, Mrs. Quah, and how you became a Christian."

"It is not a good story." Mrs. Quah settled her short body more comfortably on the sofa. "Being born to a well-to-do family, I was taught manners, but not discipline. And, being a favored one, I grew up headstrong, sometimes acting very naughtily!" Black eyes scintillated mischievously, conjuring up bygone days. A woman of culture, Mrs. Quah spoke excellent English, which she kept polished by playing the game Scrabble.

"I was born here in Thailand on the island of

Phuket. My parents named me *Paik* [white] *Hoah* [stork] symbolizing long life. I lived with my parents on my grandfather's estate by the sea. Grandfather, a wealthy man, had settled in the area called Ranong in Thailand, holding it for the Thai king, Rama V, better known as King Chulalongkorn, so the Burmese could not claim it. After sailing to China to pick up coolies, Grandfather started tin mines, to this day an important industry in Thailand.

"On one of King Chulalongkorn's occasional visits to Ranong, he jovially questioned grandfather, 'Any new children born?'

" 'Yes,' grandfather replied, 'a daughter.'

" 'I must name her!' King Chulalongkorn answered, and bestowed the newly born girl with the Thai name of Phut. The baby was my mother."

"Phut!" I savored the name. "Mrs. Quah, did you ever meet King Chulalongkorn yourself?"

"Yes, in my early childhood. Returning home from school one sultry day, I looked for my mother, but found the house strangely empty and quiet. A servant informed me that everyone had gone to my uncle's house as King Chulalongkorn was visiting.

"I was never allowed to go outside the compound alone. Nevertheless, I stole out the big iron gate and began running as fast as my short legs would go, my pigtail flying almost straight out behind me. Following the rank, open gutters along the streets, I made my way safely there.

"The heavy front door of uncle's mansion opened up to a huge entryway with carved banisters on the curved stairways leading up on both sides. Here I discovered about one hundred of my relatives, sitting on the polished floor, facing an improvised throne, in audience with King Chulalongkorn of Thailand.

"I picked out my mother sitting just a little to the right of the throne. Stepping around the relatives, I started walking toward her. 'Crawl! Crawl!' came loud whispers, even mother motioning wildly with both hands. This confused me, for I was not used to crawling to anybody. I hesitated, but didn't drop to my knees. Just then King Chulalongkorn smiled at me, saying, '*Mai ben rai.*' With all the audacity of a ten-year-old I marched to my mother's side."

I smiled at the thought of the independent little Paik Hoah and then queried, "With such an affluent background, how did you come to cross the line to what your Eastern world considers a Western religion?"

"Deep inside, I felt something lacking in the Buddhist religion. When my infant son fell ill, a friend advised me to take him to the Adventist clinic. At the entrance of the clinic I saw the doctor help a Chinese woman with bound feet into a rickshaw. I heard him tell the woman not to come to the office, that he would come regularly to her house. In those days the missionaries really inspired the people, and the doctor's humane act struck a responsive chord in my heart. Given the *Signs* magazine at the clinic, I read it with great interest, and the Bible truths became plain to me. It was the magazine and the actions of the missionaries at the clinic that swayed my heart toward Christianity."

Her words, "The actions of the missionaries . . . swayed my heart toward Christianity," stood out in bold relief in my mind. To think the actions of a missionary could turn a soul for, or against, God's great Bible truths made my heart tremble.

I was full of questions, and Mrs. Quah seemed to be in a reminiscent mood. "You came from a very well-to-do family. What brought you to come and work at BAH?"

"After the war clouds of Asia rolled away, I received from BAH visitors who had just returned to Thailand. Mrs. Waddell approached me to be dean of the newly organized class of nursing students at the hospital. I didn't dream of doing a work of this kind, but having family problems and realizing that work would help me get over them, I accepted. When I reached retirement age, the hospital manager moved me to the supposedly less-strenuous work of directing the laundry department."

Benevolent (I knew Mrs. Quah shared her meager salary through gifts of flowers, fruit, or *baht* not only with her workers but with everyone on the compound) but firm, at the age of seventy-three years she still managed the department.

"Paik Hoah!" This name rolled around on my tongue as though I were sampling its quality. "You were well named, for God has given you a long life!"

"But I am no longer the favored one. My relatives are polite to me, but they look down on my religion." Mrs. Quah gave a big sigh. "Never mind, I still love them."

"Mrs. Quah, you were God-sent to BAH! Your presence and love gifts are a continual blessing to this compound."

"I never planned to stay in Bangkok. I know Someone planned it for me, so I would be close to Christians. And how I love the missionaries!" Mrs. Quah smiled. "You have shown me the Christian way."

The hour was late. I listened to Mrs. Quah's wooden getas slowly clopping down the steps, fading into the quiet night. Paik Hoah, God's precious jewel and a legend on the BAH compound! But her childlike trust in the missionaries made me blush. Missionaries' lives pointing the way to God! It was a solemn thought.

" . . . and Gentle People"

Songkran, a purifying water ceremony in the spring, found the priests of the *wat*, as well as pious Thai people, pouring holy water on images of Buddha. To the fun-loving populace, the festival had become an excuse for throwing water on each other and any unwary passerby. At times the people's exuberance in the relaxed ritual almost approached delirium, water coming at one, seemingly from all directions!

Songkran time was a day to stay in the safety of the compound. But it was my afternoon off, and my old love for mingling with the Thai people lured me outside to a chat with Lek, my favorite beauty operator.

The shophouse beauty parlor lacked the modern facilities—my head enclosed in an ancient hair drier, wind-swept rain often dripping on me from cracks in the wall. Nonetheless, I fancied the lowly salon's caste system: the *farang* paying the full price of five *baht* (25 cents), the higher-class Thai a *baht* lower, then dropping to the servant's purse of one *baht*—everyone coming out of the shop with an equally well-set coiffure.

As Lek started combing out my hair, I queried, "Lek, your husband, have many wives?"

Like the tinkling of a bell, laughter spilled from her

lips as she raised one finger. "Me!" A triumphant note rang in her voice.

"Just you?"

Lek smiled in agreement.

"You very lucky!"

"*Mem kha*, no!" Lek shook her pretty head in emphasis. "When marry, friends say, 'Oh, he ugly! He no *baht* [has no money]! But have plan. If ugly, no women want. If no *baht*, can only have one—me! I work, too. And we happy. He good to me."

I mentally applauded Lek's ingenuity in getting around the polygamy problem, officially abolished years ago but still openly practiced.

As I left the beauty shop, an assorted crowd of Thai children congregated around me, chirping, "*Farang! Farang!*" making me an open target for the water-happy adults and their "purifying" bath. After a few purchases I caught a taxi to the compound, bypassing the local bus, for I knew the merrymakers often threw buckets of water into the open bus windows to drench the passengers!

Back at the apartment I emptied my small bag of purchases on the table. The rolls of film I'd bought in preparation for a short furlough were missing! Could the cashier have inadvertently placed them in someone else's shopping bag? I called the store. No one had reported finding the missing film. The clerk took my name and number, but I realized it was probably a lost cause.

However, the next day a man, speaking excellent English, called and said he had my film. Giving me the address of a hotel where he was staying, he made an appointment to meet me after work.

I walked into the hotel lobby that evening, and a young American GI came toward me with a package in his hand. I thanked him profusely for returning the film and started to leave.

"May I buy you a drink?" The GI pointed to a dimly lit room.

"Thank you, but no. You see, I don't drink."

"Not even water?" He joked. Then, "You're the first American woman I've talked to since leaving the States about three months ago." A note of homesickness crept into his voice. Won't you have a Coke with me in the patio?"

"Well, maybe a Seven-Up."

We sat down at a small table. Our conversation slipped into life in Thailand, his frustrations with the language, and his fondness of the gentle Thai people.

"It's too bad the Americans try to revamp the Thai style of living by sending over Peace Corps workers and missionaries."

My head shot up from looking at the frosted glass in my hand. Was he serious? But, not noticing my reaction, the GI went on talking about the Thai servants at his upcountry quarters, their uninhibited giggles and charming ways.

"Have you ever seen the servants' quarters?"

The GI shook his head.

"They may smile broadly in the daytime," I continued, "but at night they superstitiously shut the doors and windows. They sleep in the stifling heat for fear of the *pe*, their name for spirit. They believe evil spirits come in through openings, bringing disease and misfortune."

"That's only the uneducated."

"No, not really. Even the well-educated Thai people fear the *pe*." I went on to tell the GI of an experience of going to *Kao Yai* and, at the invitation of an Oriental family in Bangkok, stopping off to eat our picnic supper at their upcountry ranch. Due to car trouble, the caretaker gave us permission to stay overnight. I met the banker's wife later and thanked her for the wonderful night's sleep we had out on their moon-splashed porch.

"You slept *outside* of the house?" she cried in perfect English. I nodded, wondering what we did wrong. "We have had that place two years, but never have we stayed overnight, even *inside*, but make the tedious trip back and forth on Saturday and again on Sunday."

"Why?" I asked, still not quite sure what we had done wrong.

With an embarrassed laugh she admitted, "We're afraid of the *pe*."

The GI, his chair tilting backward and listening intently, now asked, "How long have you been in Thailand?"

"Going on ten years."

"Wow! What do you do?"

I'd been waiting for that question. "I'm a missionary."

His tilted-back chair across from me came down with a thud, and a flush spread over his face. "Say, I'm sorry for what I said about missionaries."

"*Mai ben rai!*" The Thai way of covering over embarrassing situations slipped out easily. "Like you, most people coming to this country only see the superficial veneer of the Thai populace. They don't know Thai women throw acid on their unfaithful husbands, mutilating their features for life. Or that some, whose husbands have taken another wife, douse their sleeping spouse with kerosene. Then, lighting a match to the husband, she grabs him in a fatal embrace, both becoming a human torch."

"Wow! They really do that?"

"Read the English newspaper if you want to know what's behind some of the cordial Thai smiles and fragrant leis. Don't misunderstand me; we're ashamed of some of the things that happen in our American society too. I love the Thai people. Their better nature is naturally cheerful and gentle. But many are plagued by unnatural customs of the country and their lower natures, with no higher power to free them. That's why we missionaries are here in Thailand."

It was time for me to leave. The lonely GI stood on the hotel steps and waved as I coaxed the hospital's temperamental gray DeSoto into the erratic Bangkok traffic.

Two days and I would be leaving on furlough! My typewriter clattered away as I tried to catch up on office dictation. A well-dressed Thai salesman opened the office door and asked to see the medical director. On being told he was holding clinic, the youthful salesman waved some pamphlets at me and pointed to the adjoining office. "All right if I put on his desk?" I nodded, anxious to keep at my work.

At lunchtime, while savoring every bite of the delectable mangoes that would be out of season when I returned, Rebecca called from the office. Did I know who had the medical director's dictating machine? I paused a moment before answering. "It was on the desk when I left some letters to be signed just before lunch."

"It's not there now." Rebecca's voice sounded emphatic.

"I'll be right over, Reby."

After searching and questioning, we decided the missing machine had been stolen by the Thai salesman. He had returned after I left, asking Rebecca, who worked in the back part of the room, if he could check on the material he'd left in the director's office. The crafty Thai salesman must have slipped the machine out with him, boldly calling out the cheery greeting, "*Sawaddi!*" as he went out the door.

The day of leaving became the usual hectic race with time. Chintara dropped by, her face dimpling with the good news of her friendship with Sae Tiah. Tiah, a successful Bangkok businessman and a church member, was a good friend of mine. However, it hurt me to watch him growing lax in his church attendance.

"Chintara, last time I left on home leave you felt it was not an auspicious time to be baptized because people would say you were doing it just to get in the new anesthesia class." I gently prodded, "Have you come to any decision yet?"

"*Mem kha*, if I baptize now, people will say I do it only to marry." Chintara's gaze dropped to the floor, her dimples quivered. In a halting voice she continued, "But I—I do—believe—"

Another Chintara excuse. As I left on furlough, hope still flickered in my heart that Chintara would make a complete surrender to Jesus.

Sawaddi Kha, Siam!

Returning from home leave, the jet banked sharply for the landing at Don Muang airport, affording me a Cinerama view of Krung Thep, the City of Angels. Its insides appeared overly congested with people, cars, and buildings, the outer edges skirted by rice paddies serenly reflecting a Thai-blue sky in its greenish waters. Upon disembarking, a hot Bangkok wind flaunted itself in my face, reminding me that Thailand thermometers seemed stuck at 90 degrees most of the year. A group of people waved at me from the top of the terminal building, wide-open smiles on their faces. My spirits instantly responded as the old love for the Thai people permeated my being.

On the compound, my apartment sparkled from a fresh going over by Wan Di. It was good to be home, but I sorely missed the Nelsons, who had left on permanent return. Change, my mind mused regretfully, was the pattern of one's life in the mission field. Little did I dream how drastically *change* would soon affect my life.

I ran over to the hospital and slipped unnoticed into the secretarial pool. Standing by the door, I looked over my familiar work habitat. The two Filipino secretaries, their typewriters chattering as if in competition, kept their noses to the grindstone, trying to keep up with the daily load of work. An air conditioner cooled the large room, its installation a providential result of the language barrier several months before.

Hour after hour, year after year, we secretaries had typed in a hot and stifling room. The manager agreed to our request for drapes, turning down the hint for an air conditioner. But a few days after the drapes were hung, maintenance men barged into the pool and began measuring windows. That same day an air conditioner was installed. Elated, I picked up the phone to thank the management.

"What?" the voice thundered into my ear. "I told the men to find out what it would cost to install an air conditioner, not to put one in!"

For a change, the frustrating language barrier had worked in reverse! And, gallantly, the manager allowed us to keep the air conditioner.

Rebecca glanced up from her typing and, seeing me standing by the door, clapped her hands together. "Hurrah! You came back just in time to help witness against the salesman who stole the dictating machine!"

"Oh, did they find the machine?"

"Yes, and many other things in his house that had been stolen. He used his job of selling machines as a front."

Back from furlough only two weeks, I received a phone call from the medical director early one evening at my apartment.

"Jeane, I'd like to talk to you a moment about two cablegrams I received today from Singapore." Cablegrams? The word, like a foreshadowing omen, sent a chill through my heart, a premonition that they framed a new era in my life. "Both cablegrams asked for your immediate release to be dean of girls at the Far Eastern Academy on the division compound."

Dean of girls? I could see myself having to patrol the halls after lights out, to supervise recreation periods, to sponsor school-related clubs, and to attend faculty meetings. I, who liked to go to bed with the chickens, who disliked playing games, who only tolerated clubs when necessary, and who loathed committee meetings of any kind!

The director's calm voice wedged in between the catastrophic thoughts racing through my mind. "The girls taking the secretarial course in the Philippines will be returning soon. Until then, we could operate the pool by using American supervision on a part-time basis. However, Jeane," the voice on the other end of the line sounded compassionate. "I'm only passing the call on to you. It's your prerogative to finish out the term you just started here at BAH or accept the call to Singapore."

I had learned to love the missionaries in Singapore from my previous relief period. But leave the smiling, lovable Thai people? Now I knew their likes and dislikes, their strong points and their weaknesses, their bent toward following the customs and superstitions of their forefathers. And, knowing all this, I loved them the more. Leave working for them permanently?

I longed to grasp those remaining years in Thailand, to separate, in my mind anyway, gradually from my adopted Thai race. But I knew God's biddings were enablings, and years of yielding to His call of service had formed in me the habit of flexibility. Although not wanting to leave Thailand, I was willing. My eyes grew misty as my voice barely whispered the words, "When should I plan to go?"

"They'd like for you to be in Singapore within the next week."

Change! There had been so much of it. But through all the changes of missionary life I could trace God's omnipotent hand skillfully maneuvering each situation, wanted and unwanted, for my spiritual good. All He had asked of me was a surrendered life. Why, I wondered, when it was for my good, was it so difficult to yield? I knew the answer. Self.

A stickler for the aphorism "A place for everything and everything in its place," I found moving frustrating. My household goods lay strewn over floor and furniture, awaiting professional movers to pack for shipping.

But through it all, God had not forgotten me. In my furloughing travels I had met a special friend—Paul. On arriving back in Thailand, an aerogramme from him awaited my homecoming. Paul's missionary service in Hawaii, too, was crammed with duties and frustrations, but his letters revealed God sitting enthroned in his heart. This encouraged me to accept the disappointment of leaving Thailand just three weeks after returning!

The final farewell, coming almost on the heels of the return welcome, took place where I would have chosen it—a Monday-morning worship service in the church. Together with nationals and missionaries, it held a spiritual depth the *farang* gatherings, though heartwarming in fellowship, never quite attained.

During the song service, my mind began peeling back the years to the first farewell speech I heard *Khun* Pleng, the assistant business manager, make to a departing missionary family. During the World War II years of occupation by the enemy, Pleng Vitiamyalaksana, the firstfruit of Adventism in Thailand, loyally guarded the clinic's medical equipment and supplies, carrying them out the back door as the

113

Japanese marched in the front. *Khun* Pleng had bravely withstood the vicissitudes in the mission hospital's progress and the varying temperaments of the constantly rotating missionaries with their unintentional, but abrupt, American ways. Highly respected at BAH, when *Khun* Pleng spoke, the nationals listened. He was their Thai patriarch, and I began to understand why as I listened that morning to his farewell remarks:

"Some missionaries come out to Thailand to travel and see the world. Others come out to buy Oriental things to decorate their homes. Still other missionaries come out to bring us their Western ways. But the missionary family leaving on furlough today has shown us that they did not come out for any of those reasons." *Khun* Pleng's round face, which had been turning more sober with the altering years, radiated his naturally jovial nature by a generous smile. "They came out because they love us, the Thai people.

Pleng Vitiamyalaksana had rearranged Hudson Taylor's remark that a missionary must *show* his sacrifice, not just talk it. And, unknown to *Khun* Pleng, that day a new missionary decided by God's grace to live up to a national's simple but profound portrait of a missionary!

Now, nearly ten years later, sitting on the renovated platform of the same church, I knew what *Khun* Pleng said years before was true. Love in the missionary's heart for the national could supersede any orientation course one could be taught. It could wipe out any cultural shock awaiting the missionary in a foreign field. And resounding anew through my mind was Pastor Richards' text, the golden key to a successful tour of mission duty: "I came to you . . . determined not to know any thing among you, save Jesus Christ, and him crucified." This lent the trait of flexibility to every situation—even leaving my beloved Thailand!

At the airport I stopped at the door of the plane for a lingering look at the land of never-ending summer. Here God had conceived in my heart a love, more precious than gold, for His flowerlike Thai race. Placing my hands together in a *wai*, I breathed, "*Sawaddi, Kha*, Siam!" in a last good-bye to the loving and lovable Thai people.

Epilogue

Intricate as the pieces of a jigsaw puzzle, God guided, by a knowing hand, my future. My friendship with Paul grew into a warm, mutual attraction during my deanship days at Far Eastern Academy in Singapore. Feeling his job was not finished, Paul asked me to come to Hawaii so we could get to know each other better. Six months later we were married.

Three wonderful years passed, and Paul wrote the General Conference in Washington, D.C., offering our services to the Far East on an Adventist Volunteer Service Corps basis. We left it in the Lord's hands as to where He needed us most, but in my heart there lurked a decided preference. When told we were being sent to Borneo, my hopes of working in Thailand collapsed like a pricked balloon. I was willing to go to Borneo, but disappointed.

Then, some weeks later, the GC informed us of a change in our mission. New destination! Haadyai, Thailand!

The news of our AVSC plans reached Haadyai, where a missionary doctor was setting up an English high school to prepare the Thai young people to obtain higher education in one of our English-speaking denominational colleges outside the country. Haadyai needed a teacher. Hearing of our availability and feeling my knowledge of the Thai language would be an asset to the work in Thailand, the doctor requested priority for our services. God had honored the desire which had lain quietly, but insistently, in the recesses of my heart.

"Jeane, what's Haadyai like?"

"Oh, its just a quiet, little, dusty town close to the Malaysian border."

Paul went on reading the letter from Thailand aloud. Soon one sentence caught our attention. "We'd like for our sixteen students to take typing, but we have a problem: We only have one typewriter, and that's of ancient vintage."

I laughed out loud. "The mission field hasn't changed when it comes to impossible foibles, Paul. How could we ever teach typing to sixteen students with one typewriter? Or bring fifteen more along?" My last remark reverberated in my head. Was I forgetting God's unlimited power in behalf of His work in the past?

Paul contacted a professor visiting in Honolulu after returning from Thailand. He had met the students we'd be teaching and stated their knowledge of practical English was almost nil. As to their taking typing, he advised it could only be used as a vehicle for improving their English. Nevertheless, Paul felt impressed to look into buying eight used typewriters—two typing periods would cover the sixteen students. Our faith that God was leading soared after passing through several narrow channels of trial in buying, packing, and seeing the secondhand typewriters shipped free to Thailand via air.

My roots were deep in the Thai soil, and upon arriving in Bangkok, I felt jubilant to be home again.

However, things had changed during my four-year absence. The secretarial pool hummed with the usual din of typewriters clacking out medical reports, but new faces sat behind the desks. *Khun* Vanna no longer supervised the student dormitory, but now taught in the School of Nursing. And Eyhui, married to a Christian doctor, no longer lived in Thailand.

Regretfully, one thing hadn't changed. In the hospital corridor I met Chintara. Her dimples still flashed as she talked about Sae Tiah and their children. Neither of us mentioned her aborted decision to follow Jesus all the way. But in my heart I wondered, Had the Bible truths Chintara once saw so clearly completely faded into oblivion?

While eating lunch with a missionary family, the door opened and in walked Samruay, the former priest. He took one look at Paul and exclaimed, "Oh, wonderful!" Invited to stay for dessert, Samruay accepted but seemed nervous about something. All at once he stood up, reached into his pocket and, laying a package of cigarettes on the table, burst into tears. "I bad boy now!" My heart ached for Samruay. His nature craved the spiritual things of life, but without help from God, he was powerless to save himself from the wiles of the evil world about him.

Arriving in Haadyai, we found the professor's prediction regarding the Thai student's use of the English language only too true. Given a simple command, they stared back, not comprehending. And these students were expected to accomplish four years of English high school in three years, using American textbooks! Nevertheless, within a week the pupils' responses were picking up. For the first time in Paul's teaching career, he had to caution students *not* to study so hard.

I taught the Bible and typing classes in the English high school, the latter far surpassing the professor's expectations, and ours. Tired from pushing the gray matter in their studies, the students used the typewriters as a vehicle for fun and relaxation, the top student reaching sixty-five words a minute the first school year. (No wonder God worked in our behalf to get the typewriters to Thailand!) I also taught English classes at Thep Amnuay, a Thai school with nearly a hundred students on the same compound. To be working more closely than ever before with the contagiously happy Thai people elicited a keen delight inside of me.

About five months after we arrived, the principal of the Thai school "escaped," as the sensitive Thais call getting out of an unpleasant situation without facing it. Seeing no other alternative, we moved into the principal's vacated apartment above our English high school to take over the job of supervising the Thep Amnuay School compound. With only wooden shutters for windows, a kitchen cabinet with a bumpy tin worktop, and an Eastern-style bathroom, our living quarters looked bleak. Then Paul discovered the silver lining.

"Jeane, you've always wanted a kitchen with a double sink!"

I inspected the kitchen more closely. A small kitchen sink sat under a window, and a hand sink perched on the kitchen wall near the bathroom door. With a wry smile, I replied, "Yes, Paul, but I wanted them together!" Then from the past came Hudson Taylor's remark. "You have to *show* them sacrifice." I knew my humble home appeared spacious compared to the hovels scattered around the rice fields skirting the Thep Amnuay compound.

Paul had warned me that upcountry living would be different from Bangkok. He was right. Surrounded as we were by rice paddies reflecting the blue sky, life on the compound at first glance appeared to be tranquil country living. But the upcountry Thai people were living as they had for centuries. The poor, endlessly scrounging around the compound for edible greens, shouted across the rice paddies to each other, their usually lilting language and bell-like laughter becoming loud and boisterous. And, unmindful of the hour, they tramped through our compound at midnight, laughing and talking as though it were midday.

Even more exasperating, be it a wedding, a death, a house blessing by the temple monks, or a male member of the family entering the priesthood, the fun-loving Thai celebrated day *and* night. Music, amplified through large speakers placed on a high pole, blared out in all directions for everyone to appreciate. Sometimes four or five movies, with loudspeakers amplifying the sound tracks, would be shown simultaneously in different areas of the main *wat* in Haadyai, only a block from our school.

And less than a block away were the carnival grounds, where not only movies were shown but also the ancient shadow plays, so much a part of the Thai people's way of life. These events began at sundown and ended at sunrise! Keeping track for thirty-two days, I counted twenty-four nights of continuous noise. And to think I had described Haadyai as a *quiet*, dusty little town!

I saw little of my former Thai friends. School schedules kept us busy in Haadyai. But one day I heard a familiar clopping sound on the wooden stairs outside our apartment. Then a round face appeared in the doorway.

"Anybody home?" The voice was a bit quavery, but the pixie face was that of Mrs. Quah!

I jumped up and welcomed her into our humble place. She was making an overnight stop on her way to visit relatives in Penang. Knowing that the pomelo (the Oriental grapefruit) was mostly dry and tasteless in southern Thailand, she'd carted a love gift of sweet and juicy pomelos all the way down to us. Strong in the faith, Mrs. Quah still worked at BAH at 84 years of age!

Siriporn of Phuket also made a surprise visit to Haadyai, effervescent as ever. She had grown in stature spiritually since her student days at BAH. Now working as a supervisor nurse in Phuket, off-duty hours found Siriporn helping the mission to translate spirit-of-prophecy books into the Thai language.

Our AVSC tour of duty slipped by, God being with us in a marked manner. In the outlying areas of Haadyai, Communist snipers lurked and violence erupted, while robberies and murders were common right around us. We'd been warned that men of bad reputation watched the Thep Amnuay compound. Stashed away in my traveling bag in our upstairs apartment, we kept the Thai school's tuition income, as well as the payroll for the staff of twelve teachers. Living on an open compound on the outskirts of the town, having no telephone and being the only Caucasians, we were vulernable for attack. At times hearing gunshots ring out in the middle of the night, I cowered close to Paul, our trust in an omnipotent God. He never failed us!

The last days of our appointment in Haadyai found the students keeping up with the accelerated school schedule, finishing two and two-thirds years of English high school during our two-year stay. (But even more

121

blessed would be the news a few years later that three of our four non-Adventist students had been baptized!)

Paul and I counted it a great privilege to be ambassadors for God in Thailand. Erring human beings that we were, we knew if any good came out of our overseas service, it could only be through the constant effort of yielding self. If one stayed flexible, easier said than done, one's mission, by God's grace, could transcend cultural and communication barriers.

And then the "noiseless foot of time" brought our appointment with the amiable Thai people to an end. Upon packing our few personal belongings, surges of conflicting emotions tugged at my heartstrings. My roots had crept even deeper into the Thai soil. Now etched on the tables of my heart were the upcountry people of Thailand, as loving and as needy of a way out of their problems and superstitions as the Bangkok people.

The train slowly pulled out of Haadyai. Paul and I leaned out the window as far as we dared, waving to the multitude seeing us off at the station. The familiar faces gradually melted into the lengthening distance, leaving behind the lilting tonal speech, the bell-like laughter, and the easygoing ways, all synonymous of Thailand. Again the hardest part of missionary life were the good-byes!

"Jeane." I turned tear-filled eyes to look up and found misty Thai-blue eyes looking down at me. "God willing, someday we'll come back and work in Thailand again."

Paul, too, loved Thailand? Wonder of wonders! God had woven my love affair with Thailand into a threesome—Paul and me and the lovable Thai people!